ANARCHIC ANTHOLOGY

There are authors for whom no genre properly encapsulates the nature of their anthologies. Easily distracted from any course they might choose, like the most skittish of butterflies they flit erratically and perch too briefly to be easily pinned down. Pat O'Reilly has consistently thwarted his own efforts to contain his wild imagination, thereby also subverting others' attempts to categorise his novels and short stories.

From the author whose published novels include *Harnessing the Unicorn, Frazzle,* and the winding river mystery trilogy *Dead Drift, Dead Cert* and *Dead End,* this collection of short stories includes some of his weirdest, spookiest and zaniest creations.

Anarchic Anthology

Collected Short Stories by
Pat O'Reilly

Kindle Edition first published in the United Kingdom in 2023 by
First Nature
www.first-nature.com

Second Edition Copyright © 2024 Pat O'Reilly
All rights reserved. No part of this publication may be reproduced, stored in an information retrieval system or transmitted by any means, whether electronic, mechanical, photocopying, Internet publication, recording or any other medium without the written consent of the publisher.

Pat O'Reilly has asserted his rights under the Copyright, Designs and Patents Act 1998 to be identified as the author of this work.

This is a work of fiction. Names of characters, places and businesses are either products of the author's imagination or used in a fictitious manner. Any resemblance to actual events, or to actual people, living or dead, is entirely coincidental.

CONTENTS

1. Cold Comfort 4
2. The Hole Truth 18
3. The Drop In Drop Out 19
4. Paper Trail 25
5. Angie's Aunt Lucy 28
6. Hyphen 34
7. In the Fullness of Time 38
8. Contrariwise 45
9. Pier Pressure 50
10. Star Turn 54
11. Flight of Fancy 55
12. A Window on Conscience 63
13. Fear 68
14. Villain, Victim, Victor 73
15. Melting Pot 90
16. Don't Tell the Children 93
17. No Going Back 95
18. Magic 98
19. Mark of Respect 100
20. On Reflection 106
21. A Grave Mistake 112
22. A Tissue of Truths 114
23. Sales Pressure 119
24. Flying Forever 121
25. Blue Screen of Death 123
26. Feet of Clay 130
27. Neither Friend Nor Foe 132
28. Fairy Tail-ending 140

About the author 142

1 Cold Comfort

'Gentlemen... sad news, I'm afraid. Sad, but hardly unexpected.'

The eyes of the committee were focused on the diminutive figure perched on the edge of a wheelchair. Gloria Peacock fingered the string of pearls adorning the neckline of her blue cashmere dress. She sighed and continued, 'I'm sorry to have to inform you that Miss Franklin, our poor, dear Jenny, is fading fast. But at least we can rest secure in the knowledge that during her stay here she has been free from any pain and discomfort... thanks entirely to the kind administrations of dear Dr Armitage.'

The doctor waved away the credit, but Miss Peacock persisted. 'You are too modest, doctor. *Far* too modest. And thank you too, Peter. Over the past twelve months we have all done our best for Jenny, but we must now bid farewell to someone who has meant a great deal to us. A very great deal. To think... it was only last May that we began this new phase of our work, and you won't need reminding that tomorrow is May Day. A busy year with four new cases, although perhaps we shouldn't count the Robinson case because we've had to leave that one in cold storage for funding reasons. I do hope we will be able to do something for poor Mrs Robinson before it's too late.'

For Gloria Peacock it had indeed been a busy year. And at seventy-eight - she told people sixty-one - she was performing better than ever. Better even than in either of her films. Silent movies. Real movies, where everything had to be right first time. She had been a star at twenty, playing opposite Alphonse Torrino.

Torrino! She had carried him in Island Romance. Admittedly he'd gone on to make talking pictures and heaps of money. But he would never have made it to the top without her. Alphonse had needed her in the beginning - on-stage and off. It could have been the romance of the century, but just two weeks into filming September Moonlight they had had that terrible quarrel. And all over nothing, really. But Alphonse had stormed off and told DeCruz he could no longer work with a "temperamental has-been with a scratchy, squeaky voice." He, with his nasal vowels and his silly dees for tee-aitches, criticising her voice! She had gone straight in and told DeCruz she could do *any* voice. And so she could, but he wouldn't listen. He had replaced her with Audrey Scales. Tawdry Audrey.

The film flopped, of course. Not by losing enormous amounts of money - in fact it made quite lot in the first couple of years - but it was a flop even so: nobody even mentioned it nowadays. It had never been shown on TV - at least not when she had been watching - whereas

Island Romance had been on twice to her certain knowledge. And who remembers Torrino now? Dead and buried and long forgotten – forgotten even by Tawdry Audrey, quite probably. He had been virtually a cabbage for the last ten years of his life. Where's the dignity in that? She both loved and hated him - now, as much as then. The hate would never die as long as the love survived; and, try as she would to kill it, her love for Torrino - the exciting Torrino she used to know, not the pathetic cabbage she visited in hospital towards the end - refused to lie down and die. But that suited her just fine now.

Gloria Peacock, sad and lonely star of stage and screen, had sworn never to appear in public again. She had meant it at the time, and for almost ten years she lived the life of a recluse, not filthy rich but quite well off and with a big house and a lonely, broken heart; a life without plan or purpose.

The Institute idea had been her saviour. It was easy at first, just sharing a few rooms of her home with a couple of confused old ladies - retired thespians of course - who were in need of care and comfort in their dotage. What other use had she for her wealth? She didn't worry unduly until her savings had all but been consumed. Eventually she had to sell the house and rent somewhere smaller, but it was better than admitting defeat.

But she had to admit that the whole venture would have collapsed in ruin had she not met Roger Armitage. Although unaware of the precarious financial situation, he had joined the Institute at a time when the landlord was becoming difficult over rent arrears. Gloria recalled the letter: "Charity you might be, but I am not... Thirty days to settle the account or..."

Things were very different now. Thanks to the good doctor, she was now almost a household name again. The Gloria Peacock Institute was respected and thriving. Caring for those with no one else to care. That had been her crusade then, and it was their charter now. The idea that led to the Institute's salvation had been slow in forming; but, with her name and his medical reputation, securing financial backing quickly ceased to be a problem. Government grants and annuities from film and theatrical charities supplemented the generous gifts and covenants of wealthy individuals. Now the Institute owned the land, the building, the whole lot. Everything was paid for, and they had other investments that at a pinch could just about cover the running costs. But new covenants came in every year. Money simply wasn't a problem; they could afford the best of everything, for the Institute and those who lived there.

But she had kept her vow. She no longer took acting parts; instead, she lived her roles - and not for a few minutes or even a couple of hours, but every single minute of each and every day. What greater challenge was there? That's what kept her going, kept her mind alert - not vegetating, not going the way of Alphonse Torrino, the ultimate has-been. She had been retired from the stage nearly fifty years, yet she was working every single day. Some retirement! She still chaired the executive committee - the triumvirate, she called it - Doctor Armitage, Peter Bennett and herself. A strong team.

'How long?'

'Eh? Sorry, what was that Roger?' Gloria's attention returned to the small gathering.

Roger Armitage repeated the question. 'Jenny Franklin... When?'

'Oh, er... she can't possibly last beyond Thursday.' She turned to the tall, sallow-faced man on her right. 'Service and cremation on the Monday morning, I suggest. Would you arrange things please, Peter.'

Peter Bennett nodded. 'Leave it to me. I'll get things moving before I finish today.'

Bennett knew it would mean working late, but for her he would do just about anything. It had been like that since they first met, half a century ago. In all his days as a cabbie she was the only real film star he had ever met, and he had no desire to meet another. Not then, and certainly not now. At seventeen, he had collected newspaper cuttings and photographs, the way kids do. But it had continued through his army days, long after he had grown up. After the army, he had built up his own taxi and car-hire business. Sixteen cars and a dozen full-time drivers he had at the peak, before the big boys moved in and the bottom dropped out of the market. But he had been shrewd and sold out at the right time, ending up with a nice place of his own and enough to retire on comfortably. More than enough to satisfy his simple needs - apart from the loneliness and the interminable bouts of depression. Bennett smiled inwardly, remembering the dismay he felt on hearing that the house next door had been bought by some charity for the elderly and demented. Then she had appeared, right there on his doorstep! It was still like a dream. He had kept everything, of course - the press cuttings, the photos. He had even bought a video recorder when Coral Cruise was going to be shown on TV, but by then he had the real Gloria Peacock living right next door.

At first he had just done odd jobs to help out, but when the previous administrative assistant had retired Gloria had asked him to join her team. She had asked *him*. It was incredible. In fact everything after that had seemed unreal, a dream. Armitage had quickly diagnosed the cause of his depression and as easily dealt with it. He would need the injections daily for the rest of his life, but like insulin to a diabetic that was a small price to pay for life itself. He still owned Highcroft, but he hadn't been inside it for some years. Why bother? There was no one to pass it on to. When he went it would be sold and the money would go to the Institute.

Peter Bennett came back to the present with a jolt. She was patting his hand. 'You need sleep, Peter, you almost nodded off then. Too much nightlife, perhaps?' she chided playfully.

Peter Bennett smiled shyly, unable to match her gaze. The warmth of her touch spread right through him and he felt the colour rising in his cheeks. He hesitated just a second before reaching to place his left hand on hers. A second too late: she was half way to the door. But hadn't it always been too late? Twenty years ago, well maybe, but there was no point in saying anything now. She must know, of course, but it would remain forever unspoken.

~~~

Lieutenant Colonel Gordon Franklin OBE, DSO sat on the low wooden bench, his left hand enfolding a mug of tea, now stone cold. His other hand lay gently upon the forearm of the frail old lady, his last link with the rest of humanity. Amongst dying hyacinths a bee rummaged noisily for the last drops of nectar from the fading bells. The dear old lady who had brought warmth into his life through a long cold winter was fading too, wilting visibly. A month ago she could talk. She wasn't always entirely coherent, of course, or she wouldn't have been sent there. But it was conversation of a sort, and it was for him. There was nobody else. Oh yes, occasionally someone would ask how he was, but the last thing they wanted was a real answer. "Fine thanks, and you?" That would do nicely, but certainly not, "Well, to be honest I'm not feeling too good at the moment." He could have called her Jenny - she had told him so not long after his first visit a year ago - but she was his aunt and he was happier using that title, proud of that family tie.

The letter had been waiting for him when he returned from his club and, curiosity and a healthy suspicion aroused, he had at once taken a taxi out to Rowesbury Avenue. He'd had to think it through, but that hadn't taken long. He had never heard of the Gloria Peacock Institute and no one had ever mentioned his aunt Jenny, or any other aunts or uncles for that matter. And he simply wasn't the type to be conned into handing over his nest egg to some crackpot religious cult. Anyway, it turned out that his scepticism had not been justified. He knew that now.

Far from being fanatics, they were a handful of dedicated, caring people doing a wonderful job. He had decided to help - just Jenny at first, but later he realised there must be others even less fortunate, although he hadn't seen any of the other inmates. None out in the gardens nor inside the corridors of the old Victorian mansion - they were all too frail to leave their beds. He had seen no other visitors, either, but that was hardly surprising. Hadn't Miss Peacock told him the Institute was only supposed to take people who had no living relatives who could care for them?

Alzheimer's disease was the euphemism the doctor had used. To those who live alone it will always remain the ghastly spectre of Senile Dementia. Sometimes he lay awake for hours thinking of what it must be like to be trapped, a prisoner. Not behind prison bars, but with senses diffused by lace curtains where progressively more and more layers of lace are drawn until to the outside world it is as if you aren't there at all. And *vice versa*. Who can say what goes on in such a mind? No one knows. That was why he continued to visit her. Maybe she could still hear, still see the flowers he brought, still enjoy the companionship they had shared this past year. She had told him how wonderful they all were, the doctor, Miss Peacock and the others, and how she had been made welcome there when no one else would have her. He had seen the amazing effects of the new treatment since he had first agreed to contribute towards the special diet and drug therapy. Armitage had been right. It was little short of a miracle. From an agonised, sobbing wraith she improved until, after a few weeks, she could move about in her wheelchair, talk coherently with him, laugh with him. It was expensive, but well worth it. And what better way of spending the money? He had no one to leave it too. He had given her a year of life, a quality year - admittedly at a high price, but for Jenny and therefore for him that year had been priceless.

On his first visit, Dr Armitage had shown him round. Not into the patients' rooms - they were strictly private - but everywhere else. He had seen the residents' lounge and study, the kitchens where special meals are prepared for each patient, the freezer room with a dozen large chests each bearing the name of one of the patients. He had caused some bother by asking to see inside Jenny's freezer, but eventually a key was brought up from the kitchens and the doctor undid the big brass padlock and opened the chest. Inside were layers of opaque plastic boxes, each carefully numbered and dated. 'The diets are our only secret,' Armitage had told him. 'I'm afraid I can't let you open or even touch any of the packets. They have to remain hermetically sealed until use.'

'But why not fresh food... fruit and veg?' Franklin had asked.

'Far too risky,' Armitage had replied. 'Infection. That's the real enemy. Everything is deep frozen for six months before we dare use it. We've tried every other way, and believe me this is the safest. At present it's the only way we know. Expensive, I know, but it really works.'

The doctor had closed the chest with an air of finality. But then, as if having second thoughts he had turned back to his visitor and added, 'A lot of this stuff comes from the ends of the earth - literally. You can't get it in Europe. The climate's all wrong. Tibet, China, remote mountainous areas. That's why we can't afford much of it. We couldn't even contemplate this type of treatment without financial help. It takes weeks of tests before we know exactly what a patient needs. There's nothing really clever in our method – I've never said there is. We just do the right thing for each patient and we do it properly, meticulously. Our tests are thorough and we don't cut corners on cost or time.'

Franklin had to admit that the results spoke for themselves, certainly in Jenny's case. He would never have believed it if he hadn't seen the transformation for himself. From being incoherent, almost in semi-vegetative state, she had improved to the point where, mobility excluded, she was as physically and mentally fit as he was himself. And the recovery had been sustained for the best part of a year.

The doctor had warned him that the collapse, when it came, would be just as rapid, and quite irreversible. The decline had been all of that, and Gordon Franklin knew the end must now be very near.

'I don't know if you can hear me, aunt Jenny, but I'm seriously considering your suggestion of giving Grantham to the Institute. I promised you I would make an annual contribution, and that's all arranged. Ten thousand. Rather more than we talked about before Christmas, but I can afford it. But anyway, what do I want with a big old place like Grantham with all its running costs and repair bills? I've been rattling around in it for too long already. It's about time I got a smaller place, nearer town. At least that way I'd still see a few real people now and then. Since I retired I don't suppose I've been away from the place more than a dozen times. That's not counting our little get-togethers, of course. So... you get better, d'you hear me? Then maybe we can talk it through. It's a good thing you got me thinking about the future, though. You know how I tend to let things drift. I might easily have passed on without sorting out some worthwhile future for the family home. Hell of a shame if that had happened.'

The old lady turned her dim eyes towards him, but no hint of emotion showed on her face. He squeezed the thin arm gently, and felt her frail body shudder. Perhaps she could still feel something. Perhaps she was trying to say something. Colonel Franklin straightened himself and at once felt the chill around his own ankles. Tipping away his unwanted drink, he turned the wheelchair towards the house and said, 'We had better get you inside before the dew falls. There could even be a frost tonight. Clear sky, no wind.'

Jenny did not reply. She had talked a great deal until a month or so ago, mainly about his parents and about Grantham. Amazingly, she was able to describe every little nook and cranny, and he could sense that the old home held some very special memories for her. That was how he had come to know for sure, come to trust her judgement. Never a selfish word, always thinking of others, that was Jenny. You don't meet many people like that, not nowadays, he had concluded. She spoke only once about his father, and about the awful tragedy. How his mother had waited for news. The ship had gone down with all hands. Two days of news coverage, then long years of struggle to support herself and young Gordon. From Jenny he learned a lot about his mother that he had never known or had remembered only vaguely. He'd hardly known her as a person. She had died when he was eighteen, but the stroke five years earlier had cheated them of any real relationship. He was fourteen when she came out of hospital, and he had left school that summer, working during the day and caring for her at nights. It hadn't been hard work, just lonely and thankless. She had never improved. He hadn't felt bitter or deprived, not then at least. He had his work, and he became good at it, very good, which gave him a great start when he entered the army. His advancement had been purely on merit, he told himself with pride.

Jenny had said very little about herself. Something about her own work as "wardrobe" in a provincial theatre, nothing at all grand; about her feelings when she had to leave her own home and enter the Institute; how she had feared that once her savings were all gone she would be shuffled off into one of those cold, cramped, impersonal places you hear about so much; and how grateful she was to him and how she looked forward to his weekly visits. Now Aunt Jenny spoke no more. She no longer smiled, but gazed blankly at an unreflecting world. Lately she didn't respond when he squeezed her hand. He knew she was dying. But he would always come, always, until the end. And then...

A lump came to his throat, borne by a selfish thought: he would have no one then... alone again. 'Please don't go,' he whispered, searching her frozen gaze for some sign of understanding. A tear welled up in the corner of his aunt's unseeing eye. Then it was gone... sucked back into the tear duct. Imagination? It had to be. He shook his head. Impossible, she couldn't have!

He knelt before her, trembling, his hands gripping the wheels of her chair so tightly that the knuckles shone white, reflecting the last of the dying sun into the dead eyes of Aunt Jenny.

'I've decided,' he said. 'I am definitely going to do it. For you and for all the other people like you. And who knows, maybe one day I could be one of them. But I'm doing it for you, Jenny. It's all I can do.'

Gordon Franklin bit on his lip. Rising unsteadily, he started towards the ramp leading into the house. 'They'll be bringing your tea in a few minutes,' he told her. 'You must be famished. I can't stay long tonight, but perhaps we can have a trip out next Saturday. I'll try to come a bit earlier. How about a picnic if it's fine?' But he knew that she could have little or no awareness of hunger or thirst.

As Franklin was leaving, Armitage caught him in the corridor.

'Look,' the doctor said. 'You've been a tremendous help, but there really is no point any longer. I'm afraid there's nothing more we can do now except to make her comfortable until... But thank you, colonel. We get very few visitors here. You see, usually our people have no living relatives – it's a rule of the Institute. But Gloria - Miss Peacock - will have explained all that, I'm sure.'

Colonel Franklin nodded and the doctor continued, 'You've been marvellous. Really you have. Your visits have made a world of difference for our Jenny. And the treatment, of course. Much as we might wish it, the Institute could never afford anything like that from its own resources. You have given her the best part of a year - and a year of really living, not just existing. She's been happier this last twelve months than... well, who can say? She cried a great deal when she first came to us, you know. Said she was afraid. She wouldn't say what she was afraid of, though. We'll never know now, will we? The secret's going to the grave with her, poor dear.'

'Thank you, doctor. And remember, I do want to be called, whatever the time. She asked, so I must be there. You've got both my phone numbers.' It was a statement not a question, but Armitage reassured him, just the same.

~~~

Slim, raven-haired with lively blue eyes, Mary Armitage seemed to have the secret if not of eternal youth then certainly of eternal middle age. At sixty five she breezed along, feet almost dancing as she entered the committee room and parked herself at the head of the long oak table.

'Morning! Sorry I'm late. Gloria sends her apologies - tied up with the grants people. Shall we start? Usual format. Peter?'

So efficient, thought Armitage. He had always admired, even envied, her dynamism. She was one of the world's real achievers. Not the warmest of women, perhaps, but not *without* compassion. Thoughtless, not heartless. Yes, that was it, thoughtless, and perhaps a little selfish at times. But Mary had never intentionally hurt him - nor anyone else, to his knowledge. Career-wise he hadn't done badly himself, but he was more proud of her and happy to play a supporting role when she was around. And hadn't he every right to be proud? She'd received her training under him - his star pupil - and had gone on to become a first-class neurosurgeon, one of the country's top consultants. But he had been lucky, very lucky. He had almost lost her. Right at the pinnacle of her career something had gone terribly wrong. Almost overnight she had changed: forgetting names, missing appointments, turning up at the wrong hospital. At first he had tried to cover up for her, but it soon became hopeless. She was forced to take early retirement, give up lecturing, resign all her committee posts. Within six months she could no longer dress herself and her speech was almost unintelligible. He had to do everything for her, and soon it became too much for him. Reluctantly he had decided she would have to go into a home, and that meant he would have to go with her. Someone had mentioned that the Gloria Peacock Institute was looking for a medical director, and he had applied, insisting that admission of his wife should be a condition of the contract. Gloria told him later that it had been the deciding factor - that and his age. She hadn't wanted a young man. The work needed a "mature approach" - that's what she had said.

Then came the miracle, and he owed it all to Gloria Peacock. Without her he would have lost his Mary. The solution, when they found it, had been nothing short of dramatic. In no time Mary was fit and well, joining him in his work at the Institute whenever she could, re-building their social circle as her voice gradually returned to normal. Of course, there was no question of her returning to her professional work, but she played a key role in the running of the Institute, often deputising for Miss Peacock - as indeed she was now.

'Sorry, what was that?' Bennett replied, absentmindedly.

'Your report, Peter. Oh, for goodness sake do pull yourself together. It's not too hot in here for you, is it?'

How Peter Bennett dreaded those meetings chaired by Mrs A! She confused him. Outwardly she was so similar to his beloved Gloria - small and slim, brimming with vitality. But how could she be so unkind? It was a personal vendetta just stopping short of merciless cruelty, for there was always some substance to her criticism, some hook on which to hang the insults, the ridicule. Never pleased with his achievements, unforgiving of his failures, she could make his smallest slip appear a major blunder. Most of all he hated it when she turned those piercing blue eyes on him, blazing with a pent-up anger that surely could not be for him. It must be for someone else, he thought, someone in her past. He was thankful that Gloria chaired most of the meetings. He would have been devastated if she had spoken to him like that. But she wasn't like that.

'Sorry, Mrs Armitage. Well, nothing really. Nothing new, that is. Miss Peacock says I'm likely to be very busy this weekend, and she's not often wrong. Might have something for you by Saturday evening. If not, then definitely by the meeting after that. Monday, did you say? Or was it Wednesday?'

'I didn't say, actually. But yes, back to normal next week. I'll be chairing the Monday session as far as we know at the moment. No progress at all, then! So what have you been doing, Peter?'

Bennett shifted uneasily in his seat. 'Look, there's no need to... I've got several feelers out. I'll be seeing Social Services later today. It sounds quite hopeful, actually, but if not I've still got several other irons in the fire and...'

Mrs Armitage waved impatiently. 'For heaven's sake, Peter. Either you've got something to report or you haven't. Which is it?'

'Sorry... nothing. Nothing yet.'

'Right! Roger... anything?'

'No. Nothing new from me.'

'Well then, let's leave it at that for now. No point in opening the ledger today.'

Peter Bennett was first to reach the door. Over his shoulder he called, 'Any idea what's for dinner?'

The doctor took up the cudgel. 'Peter! It's Wednesday! Wake up, old fruit. Cook's night off, remember?'

Armitage's disgust was very thinly disguised. He shook his head and added, 'Sorry, old chap. Didn't meant to criticise. Look, Mary and I have booked a table at Burridges. Care to join us? You'd be most welcome.'

'Kind of you both,' Bennett replied. 'I appreciate it, really I do, but you can't have had much time together lately, and honestly there's loads I need to get done. Loads. I think I'll just settle for a sandwich in my room. D'you mind awfully?'

'Of course not, Peter. You suit yourself. Goodnight.'

～～

She lay there, motionless, as she had since Gordon Franklin's arrival half an hour ago. The wide blue eyes stared through him towards the open window and the evening sunset. Armitage put down the newspaper and took her pulse once more. This time he straightened and put his hand on Franklin's shoulder. The younger man jerked to full consciousness and tried to rise but fell back under the weight of a restraining hand.

'She's gone,' Armitage whispered. 'Couple of minutes ago, I would say. She's at peace now.'

Colonel Gordon Franklin fought back a tear. No silly talk about a "blessed release". He should be thankful for that. Armitage understood. Not everything, perhaps, but he understood how important Jenny had become to him. Leaning forward, the colonel brushed back a straying lock of fine white hair from the forehead of the dear old lady, the aunt he had known for barely a year. Gone forever... his last real link with the rest of humanity.

'Thank you,' the colonel said. 'Is there anything I should be doing? The arrangements and all that. It will cost money... the funeral and all that. I shall pay for everything, of course.'

'Thank you, colonel. And we are very grateful for your covenant. We could hardly ask for more. Miss Peacock will make all the arrangements. I'm afraid that's something we have to get used to in our line. You just leave it all to us. Monday, I expect. Anyway, we'll keep you informed, I promise.'

There was nothing more to say. Nothing anyone could say, or do. It was over.

～～

The committee met for the third time in a week. 'Your report first, Peter. Okay?'

'I just want to say I think you're a genius!' The thin man's face turned from parchment to pink, and he leafed through the blank pages of his desk pad as if searching for something. 'Sorry,' he continued, still not looking up. 'Er... twenty-three... let's see now. Yes. Well, things are moving at last. I know we don't want to count our chickens before they're...'

'Peter!' Momentarily Peter Bennett closed his eyes and held his breath, but it was Gloria, not Mrs A. 'The facts first, please. Just the facts for now, Peter dear.'

'Of course... the facts.'

Armitage launched an impatient glare at the man sitting beside him, but Peter Bennett was still shuffling blank papers. 'Ah, yes. Got it here,' he went on. 'Forty-five thousand for special diet and treatment. Then there's the covenant, as you know. Ten thousand a year for a minimum of five years. Might have been fifteen, but never mind. And there's a bonus. We had just about written off the manor house, but I heard from Gibbons and Jackson this morning. We're not yet supposed to know officially, but we've got it. The papers will take a while to come through, but in all that makes three hundred and fifty thousand plus.'

'A third of a million,' Armitage muttered. 'Not bad!'

Gloria Peacock opened the ledger. 'Gentlemen...' She glanced around the room and smiled. 'Twenty-three projects completed. Total income four and a half million, leaving just under three million clear after costs. Not bad at all. We'll reach our five million target this year, I'm sure. Quite a milestone, but we owe it all to the likes of dear Colonel Franklin.' She paused to smile across the table at her colleagues. 'A worthy cause. What better way could they spend the money?' The others nodded approvingly, and she continued, ''Now then, Peter, back to work. What else have you to report. Any fruits from your researches?'

The thin man opened a folder - real notes this time - and glanced at them briefly. 'Yesterday morning I arranged for a Miss Kendall - Miss Elsie Kendall - to be transferred here.'

Roger Armitage stiffened in his chair, and Bennett glanced up nervously. Perhaps he should have consulted the committee. But it was his job to find needy cases, to do all the checking and gather the vital little details. And he knew he was good at it; she had said so. He'd had no option but to make a snap decision on the Kendall case, otherwise the dear old soul might have been carted off to Downlands. He had acted quickly, decisively. Gloria would approve.

'Anyway,' Bennett continued, 'I've been looking into this one for some weeks. I've done a full check, otherwise I'd never have said we'd take her, you know that. She's got no one, I'm sure. Not a living soul. Except, that is...' Bennett paused and swung his gaze across the expectant faces now concentrating intensely on him. 'Except, that is, for a Miss Anthea Kendall-Rothman, a cousin.'

Gloria was pleased! She was smiling at him. 'Anyway, as I was saying,' he went on, more confident now, 'she's been in Gladeview - Miss single-barrelled Kendal that is - for the past ten years or so, but now they say they can't cope with her. Too costly in staff time is the real reason, of course. We all know what Anne Phillips runs that place for.'

Two heads nodded as one. Two faces reflected their disdain for mercenary so-called rest homes.

Enthusiastically now, Bennett completed his report. 'Couldn't do a thing for herself, poor soul. Wheelchair... Doubly incontinent...' He waved an expansive et cetera, shrugged his shoulders and added, 'I've done the usual photos and video clips, so how about a first dress rehearsal tonight, just in case the Social people come early. They came the very next day with Pru Robinson. Remember? What a bloody scramble that was. Not at all nice.'

'Oh you're so right, Peter dear. I won't have the Institute run like some amateur show.'

Gloria Peacock's eyes were lit up. The first dress rehearsal was always exciting. The day it wasn't she would retire, but she prayed never to see that day dawn.

The medical man took over. 'I'll see to her right away. She can have Jenny's freezer.'

'Well done, everyone,' Miss Peacock said. 'Now then, Peter... What can you tell us about this Miss Rothman-Kendall?'

'Er... the other way round. The Kendall first. But don't worry, you'll have my full report. It's almost finished and everything you need is in there.'

Peter Bennett thumbed back through his folder. 'Right, then,' he continued. 'Briefly... she's a senior partner in Milton, Fielding and Rothman, solicitors. Branches all over the South. Head office in the city. Her old man was one of the founders. She's been there since the year dot. Should have retired years ago, by all accounts.' Bennett shrugged. 'You know how it is. Usual story... nothing else outside of her work. Rents a flat in town, but she's got a nice place in the country, just outside Lower Bardsley. Hardly ever there, though. Spends next to nothing on herself. It's all in the report. See what you think.'

~~~

Gloria Peacock spun her electric wheelchair in a tight circle before closing the report with a flourish. Her big blue eyes sparkled with excitement. 'Two minutes to ten! Everybody ready? Now remember, Peter, when you take her from my office you must walk more slowly through the grounds. You really must take your time, dear.' Her eyebrows disappeared under a silk headscarf, as a new and more serious voice took over. 'If Elsie Kendall isn't ready on cue, the show folds, right there and then. Oh, and what about her lovely new wheelchair. It's motorised!' A smile lit up her face. 'Oh... will I need a driving licence, Peter?'

<center>~~~</center>

As Anthea Kendall-Rothman climbed the stone steps leading to the half-open oak doors of the Gloria Peacock Institute, laughter echoed along the corridor from a room outside which hung a label saying, "Committee Meeting in Progress". Not at all the chilling, impersonal kind of place she had feared.

-oo0oo-

2 The Hole Truth

Life on an overcrowded island inevitably involves compromise. He accepts that. Green space is at a premium, and hence very few couples have the luxury of a brand new home. The majority have to settle for temporary, refurbished accommodation - a DIY challenge that some couples are faced with nearly every year.

This time his partner had found them something different, something special: a spacious, repurposed home in which to bring up a family. They had snapped up the opportunity ahead of many other bidders.

Inevitably there has been a lot of work to do to get the place up to a reasonable standard. The previous occupants had left it in a bit of a mess, and so he and his partner have labouring long and hard to clear out all the junk, to get the place clean, and to turn it into a neat and tidy family home.

While his partner has been putting the finishing touches to their new abode, he has been working away, toiling long hours, determined to ensure that they both have plenty of wholesome food to eat. After all, she is no longer eating just for one.

On his way home in the warm May sunshine, among all the bluebells and red campion that border their home a solitary primrose catches his eye. Today he will not pick her a posy but just that one pretty flower. She will love it.

Undeterred by the curious gaze of onlookers, he plucks the primrose and carries it carefully to the entrance of their new home. A quick glance to left and right, and in he goes.

What finer love token could a puffin take to the beautiful bird who awaits him in their Skomer Island rabbit-hole home?

-oo0oo-

3   The Drop In Drop Out

A wild wind rattled the roof tiles, as torrential rain turned west-facing windows into waterfalls. It was, Cicely Walker decided, a stay-at-home evening if ever there was one. She had very few visitors nowadays, and on a night like this she hadn't been expecting anyone to drop in. But Mort did.

In fact Mort Wellow was the last person she would want to see, in fair weather or foul. Their constant feuding was legendary around the parish of Sheckford. Nothing was more certain to raise the hackles of either than the merest mention of the other. Figurative hackles, in Mort's case, as it would have taken supernatural powers to raise the tangled ropes of grey hair that hung like shower curtains from the sides of his shiny dome. "Fronds of dead seaweed storm-strewn on a barren shore," Cicely had once called them.

Mort set his own standards. She could say what she liked, pompous old prune! He didn't need lessons in personal hygiene from that old windbag. He washed regularly. And every Sunday before church his razor fought a bloody battle to unmask features moulded by the passage of time, and re-moulded by the passage between Mort's sitting room and his kitchen, with whose low doorway he frequently collided. He really would fix it one day. But time was a great healer, and by mid-week his ruddy face was back behind its familiar screen of dapple-grey stubble.

Mort Wellow liked peace and quiet, the countryside and animals. And beer! He didn't much like work. He did a few odd jobs on farms around Sheckford, fixing a broken hinge here, a damaged fence there; mucking out a barn, a stable, a sty. There was always plenty of mucking out. He'd do an hour a day - two at the most. Just enough for his beer money; Mort Wellow had few other wants.

Old Mort lived alone in a ramshackle cottage on Tanner's Hill, two miles from Sheckford village. The cottage had been left to him by an aunt some thirty years earlier, and on coming into his inheritance he had at once moved out of Riverlea, the Wellow family home in the village centre. Mort's old place had stood empty since the day he left. Twelve years ago he had almost killed himself trying to replace a couple of slipped roof slates, and thereafter Riverlea had remained locked and shuttered. The Walkers had tried to buy it when illness forced Reverend Walker to retire from the vicarage. Mort wouldn't even consider the matter.

'Riverlea's for me retirement,' he had told them. 'For when I can't make it no more up Tanner's 'ill. Comes to us all in time, your reverend - no disrespect intended'.

Three years in a row Sheckford's entry in the county's Best Kept Village competition had been undermined by the appalling state of Riverlea. In the end the campaign organiser had decided that further entries would be '...habsolutely pointless huntil Riverlea falls down hentirely'.

It was true: the 'front lawn' at Riverlea produced enough dandelion seed to keep the gardeners of Sheckford fully occupied; and in the back garden adjoining the riverside park, nettles and brambles fought over heaps of rusting farm machinery. But, on balance, the villagers were glad that Mort Wellow had chosen to live on a high and windy hill. Often there would be debates as to whether, were it not for the cleansing rain and strong winds over Tanner's Hill, anyone could survive at ten paces the intense odour that accompanied Mort everywhere he went.

Everywhere, for Mort, meant to church on Sundays and to The Three Curlews most other days. But the people of Sheckford were considerate folk: none would have dreamt of raising the matter with Mort for fear of hurting his feelings.

None, that is, except Cicely Walker.

As they left the church each Sunday, parishioners were greeted not by the vicar but by Cicely. This responsibility she had assumed when her husband had been vicar of Sheckford, and she had continued to discharge it with dignity and diligence for the twenty years since his death. For each member of the congregation, villager and outsider alike, she had a few kind words.

Except for Mort Wellow.

Cicely Walker's greeting for Mort was always the same, and delivered with unremitting venom: 'You stink, Mortimer Wellow. What you need is a hard scrub with carbolic soap.'

In return Mort would smile and raise his nose to the sky: 'I can't smell nothin' bad over 'ere where I am, Mrs Walker.' Then he would edge towards her, all the while sniffing the air. That was her signal to retreat to the vestry and tidy up after the vicar.

~~~

Cicely Walker loved order and routine. Inside, Number Two, The Terrace everything was always spotlessly clean and perfectly tidy: no magazines open on the polished table, no cushions scattered at random on the chintz three piece suite. A place for everything, and everything in its place. But a place in Cicely Walker's home, as in her life, had to be earned. For dust there was no place; nor, indeed, for a cup or saucer with the slightest crack or chip. Outside, the windows sparkled. The slate steps from the road down to the front door shone in sun or rain, their treads worn more by the last twenty years of daily burnishing than by three centuries of feet tripping down to the cosy little front room.

Villagers and visitors were treated alike. The penalty for dropping a bus ticket was an immediate confrontation with Cicely Walker's accusing eyes. The old lady would spring from her lair, swoop on the offending paper and return it to the miscreant with: 'Is this something valuable you've dropped, or were you trying to dump your rubbish houtside my home?'

Nobody who knew her dropped litter while Cicely Walker was around. Nor aitches - that was something else she pounced upon. And perhaps it was her intense dislike of waste that compelled her, having picked up so many of other people's dropped aitches (haitches, she called them), to re-cycle them ostentatiously at every opportunity.

~~~

But back to that stormy Saturday night. As usual, Mort had been the last to leave The Three Curlews. His lurching gait would add a good half mile to the journey home, by which time he would have sobered up enough to shoo the chickens into the back room, make himself a strong mug of tea, set his alarm clock and climb into bed.

Had the landlord of The Three Curlews been in less of a hurry to escape the driving rain, he might have seen Mort clutch the bus stop and swivel around it, twirling one way, then the other, hooting with joy as he had for nearly sixty years - the last twenty to the intense annoyance of Cicely Walker, who sat glowering in her easy chair. Every night she would put away her knitting as soon as The Three Curlews closed and Mort Wellow lurched past her window and away to Tanner's Hill; never before.

'We-hey!' Mort spiralled round the bus stop, sinking slowly towards the ground until his fingers slipped from the cold metal. He spun away clutching at thin air, slithered across the footpath, down a flight of steps and into a dark abyss.

Thud! Mort Wellow's head bounced against Cicely Walker's oak front door.

'You're drunk, Mortimer Wellow, you reprobate. Get hoff home with you!'

~~~

Sunday service at Sheckford Parish Church was always well attended. The same could not be said of the two other parishes on the circuit. Late risers would travel across from Melkton and Wooton, whose services began at eight o'clock and nine-thirty. By the time he got round to Sheckford at eleven, the vicar was beginning to wilt and his sermon was invariably brief and to the point. The faithful could be back home in time to cook the Sunday lunch or, as in Mort's case, down at The Three Curlews by opening time.

By tradition, first into church was Mort Wellow, Sheckford's most senior citizen, taking up his rightful place in the front row at the left. His was the pew right beside the aisle. Although late for every other engagement he was always up early on Sundays, and he hadn't missed a service in over sixty years. His name was on his pew - indeed, so were the names of all of Sheckford's regular churchgoers. This practice had been established in the late Reverend Walker's time, and no one seemed minded to change it.

The congregation would trickle in and take their seats. Now and then an inquisitive choirboy would peer around the vestry door, but the service itself would not start until the churchwarden had taken up her rightful place. That place, in the front row on the right, beside the aisle, bore a brass label inscribed "Mrs Cicely Walker".

On this particular Sunday something was very wrong. The storm of the previous night had died down and from time to time the sun peered cautiously from behind drifting shower clouds, mimicking the antics of the choirboys now taking it in turns to recce every thirty seconds. Worried murmurings echoed in the arches of the old Norman church. Feet shuffled uneasily and heads swivelled to scan the back of the porch. Where was Mort? His pew remained empty, incongruous, a black tooth defiling the smile of a Carnival Queen. Eventually, just two reserved places stood vacant: those of Mort Wellow and Cicely Walker. No one worried about Cicely: the church would have been locked if she hadn't arrived. But what about Mort? He had seemed his usual self in The Three Curlews the night before, sprawled in his customary fireside chair with a tankard of beer and injecting the occasional irrelevance into whatever conversation drifted to his ears.

By five past eleven the elders of the parish had come to a decision. Someone would have to go up to the cottage on Tanner's Hill. A farmer's son was sent to investigate and to leave a message at The Three Curlews to set everyone's mind at rest. Or otherwise. They had to face that possibility. Mort was no spring chicken.

As the emissary was leaving he almost collided with a late arrival, a man from outside the area. You could always tell outsiders: they would hover in the porch, unsure whether to take one of the vacant pews at the front or stay near the door where they could slip out unnoticed if the sermon overran.

The newcomer, a plumpish man, probably in his seventies, well dressed in a black two-piece suit, starched collar and grey tie, looked around uncertainly. His sparse grey hair glistened in the sunlight that streamed through the open door. Then he strode swiftly to the front of the church and knelt in one of the labelled pews. Mort's pew!

The murmuring rose in intensity, there was a dull thud followed by muffled groans as the heads of two inquisitive choirboys collided, but no one came forward to explain to the visitor. How could they? The service would have to start soon, and Mort still hadn't arrived. Of course, the occupant of Mort's pew would have to be moved; Cicely Walker would have to sort it out. A reserved pew is a reserved pew, to be filled only by the person whose name is on the brass label. Until that person dies, that is, and then the label is transferred to their coffin and the next most senior parishioner is moved forward. That's how things were done in Sheckford Parish Church: an orderly procedure, supervised personally by Sheckford's most orderly churchwarden.

Suddenly lips froze in mid whisper. Feet stopped in mid shuffle. In the doorway stood Cicely Walker. She hung up her umbrella, adjusted an errant hatpin and paused until her eyes grew accustomed to the dim interior. Her gaze swept across the congregation, finally settling on the stooped figure in the front left aisle-side pew. The faithful of Sheckford and district held their breath as Cicely Walker strode purposefully down the aisle, drawing up beside the man in Mort Wellow's place. She looked down at the bowed figure. He did not look up. For a brief instant a benevolent smile seemed to light up her wrinkled face (years later villagers were still arguing whether it had been a trick of the light), and then she turned to the right, settled behind her labelled pew and nodded towards the vestry door. The vicar entered, took three paces towards the alter and came to an abrupt halt, his eyes darting repeatedly between the intruder in Mort Wellow's pew and the old lady on the opposite side of the aisle. One of the choirboys, caught unawares, bounced off the vicar's thigh and slewed to a halt before the altar steps, remaining upright only by an impressive feat of acrobatics. Again Cicely Walker nodded to the vicar.

It was as if her gesture had cleared a blockage in the sands of time. The scene unfroze and the service proceeded. With an *ad lib* adjustment to his sermon, the vicar of Melkton, Sheckford and Wooton brought the proceedings to a close at eleven-forty precisely, and the congregation filed from the church. As usual, Cicely Walker greeted each with a smile and a few words of encouragement.

'Mrs Steadman... I'm so glad you're well henough to join hus again. Ah, Miss Phillips. I got your message. So good of you to hoffer to help at the fete. I'll let you have hall the details next Sunday.' And for the old man who had usurped Mort Wellow's pew she had a particularly warm smile: 'Do drop in again. Hanytime.'

The man made no reply, but sped away without once looking back.

~~~

In contrast to his surprisingly sudden departure, Mort's return, both to Sheckford and to his own brand of normality, can only be described as… gradual.

-ooOoo-

4 Paper Trail

DIY was not his greatest strength, but Jim Sandcraft was strapped for cash. Buying the derelict old farmhouse had consumed not only his redundancy lump sum but also a large part of his modest life savings. Whatever needed fixing he would do it, or it would have to remain undone. As a long-term prospect it was too remote and isolated. He knew that. But he had convinced himself that he could reasonably expect to cope alone there for ten, fifteen, maybe even twenty years. Years of peace and the kind of solitude he had always craved. Here, once the place was habitable, he could carry on tutoring would-be novelists a couple of days a week, and the rest of the time he would be free. Free to wander, to wonder, and to get back to writing. His reputation as a creative writing tutor stemmed almost entirely from *Hell's Hidden Horrors*, J M Sandcraft's first and so far only novel. Still in print after 22 years but now with dwindling sales, its royalty cheques were no longer the major income boost they had once been. His second book would also be a thriller, of course. But so far he hadn't even been able to dream up an intriguing title, never mind a theme or the basis of a plot. But he would. His publisher had been nagging him for years, but Jim's muse was a mule, stubbornly refusing to work around real-life interruptions. As soon as he could sort out the house, he would get down to some serious writing.

Two or three months of hard graft should get the lounge, kitchen and one bedroom to a reasonable standard. That's all he needed. Meanwhile, he was camping in the kitchen with the windows wide open. Only there, with a stone floor rather than damp carpets, could he breathe without feeling sick. At least the slate roof was sound, and the windows had hardwood frames that looked good for quite a few more years. The most important thing was to use the warm summer months to dry the place out and get rid of the awful stink left by a flash flood. Muddy water had poured in through the back door and out through the front, which was the main reason that no one else had been interested in buying the smelly old farmhouse. The fields once belonging to the holding had been sold off years ago, which was the other reason Jim had been able to afford the place; the plot was so small you could either park a car or grow a few herbs in pots, but not both.

Many years after buying the fields, the neighbouring farmer had also obtained ownership of the old ruin via the Adverse Possession rule. The farmer's death three years ago had eventually triggered the sale, but it had also closed the most obvious door to the history of the old house, a subject which Jim Sandcraft hoped one day to have time to research.

Before the autumn, Jim would dig a trench around the back and sides of the house, as recommended in a guide to flood-risk management that he had found online. But first he had to do something about that vile stink.

Mouldy carpets. Just getting *them* out of the lounge ought to make a big difference, so that's where he would start. Using a kitchen knife to make a long slit across the middle of the room, Jim levered up a ragged edge of carpet and peered beneath. The masthead of **THE OBSERVER** newspaper stared back at him. It was dated 20 July 1969, and below its familiar lion-and-unicorn logo was the proud proclamation *Established 1791*. The top-of-the news headline read: **Apollo 11 rockets into moon orbit**. Jim Sandcraft knew the rest of that story very well; he had been born just moments after Neil Armstrong had stepped onto the surface of the moon. Further down the front page in much smaller print he saw: *Girl in Kennedy's Car Drowns*. The moon landing had all but buried the news of Mary Jo Kopechne's death when Senator Edward Kennedy's car ran off a bridge at Chappaquiddik.

Jim's carpet clearance revealed more makeshift underlay, including a further 30 *Guardian* and *Observer* front pages all dated 20 July. The latest, *The Guardian* of Tuesday 20 July 1999, led with news that two former senior police officers were to be tried for manslaughter in connection with the 1989 Hillsborough disaster. The rest of the underlay was an assortment of *Radio Times* and celebrity gossip magazines. But Jim's biggest surprise came when he managed to decipher the faint pencilled inscription on each of the Guardian and Observer front pages. *To JMS, Happy Birthday from Auntie Marlene and Uncle Tom.* He was James Martin Sandcraft, but he knew of no aunts or uncles on either side of his parents' families. He shrugged. Coincidence, nothing more. Back to work…

More carefully now, he tore back the rest of the carpet and carefully slid his knife beneath each of the newspapers. Lifting them more or less intact, he spread them out to dry on every flat surface he could find. If nothing else they would be a fascinating source of topics to challenge his students with. But then, as he worked to cut up the carpet into manageable pieces, his mind wandered off into plotting mode. Who was the mysterious JMS with whom he shared a birthday? Could it be that he or she had also been born on moon-landing day? Probably not, if they were expected to read the first half dozen newspapers sent as birthday presents. So what happened to stem the tide of yearly souvenirs? Instantly rejecting any credible and innocent explanations, Jim's scheming mind wondered whether JMS had murdered the aunt and uncle. If so, why? Or had they murdered *him*? And where were the bodies buried? Was that terrible smell due solely to the rotting carpet? Or, concealed beneath the floor of this derelict old farmhouse that had been uninhabited for years, was there something else? Something or someone!

Jim Sandcraft decided to do a bit more digging, starting with the lounge floor. Whatever the outcome, he now had a theme and the main characters - the basis of his new thriller. He even had a title: *The Bare Bones of a Plot*.

-ooOoo-

5 Angie's Aunt Lucy

It would never have happened if Angie's Aunt Lucy had remembered to clip the wings of her chickens before school closed for the summer.

'Heaven knows how they can tell, but chickens know to the very day when term ends and the holidays start,' Angie's Aunt Lucy had told me on numerous occasions. 'Especially the hens. There's nothing they like better than lots of things going on in the park. Lots to gawk at.' I had no reason to doubt her. After all, she had been right about the outcome of World War Two - she told me so herself.

Many a time Angie's Aunt Lucy had held us spellbound with tales of spilt water bowls, of hens running amok, scratching whenever and wherever they pleased and without so much as a by your leave; of hens in the wrong pens - even clucking after lights out! The Ragged Old Cockerel got so distressed that he spent most of the summer holidays cowering in a vacant nest box, creeping out nervously only at meal times. I suggested the constant influx of footballs, kites and other missiles from the park might have been a contributory factor, but Angie's Aunt Lucy would have none of it. She was adamant it was mass hysteria transmitted by telepathy from child to child, child to chicken, chicken to chicken.

But of course, all this boisterousness was bound to end in tears. And recently it did. In a moment of youthful exuberance one of the hens flew up over the wire netting and into the alder tree beside the duck pond. Perched precariously on a branch overhanging the pond, it took fright and simply refused to come down.

She wouldn't come down for corn; she wouldn't come for bacon rind; she even refused the bribe of a piece of crispy golden chicken skin. And when a chicken won't come for roast chicken you know it's *really* scared. But Angie's Aunt Lucy said it was quite understandable. A hen with vertigo can't do a thing; it simply freezes with terror.

'Of course, they're not naturally cannibal,' Angie's Aunt Lucy would assert in their defence. 'Really, you know, they're all very much like me.'

I hadn't thought of it before, but when she had raised the matter I could see similarities: piercing, flickering round eyes set in a small flattened head - a head perched, often askance, on a scrawny, telescopic neck where she kept all her spare skin, certainly enough to cover two or three such necks. Bodily similarities were less specific: a gangling, bony frame of uncertain proportions concealed beneath layers of plumage which varied little with the seasons; a rump always well in arrears, she moved like 'poultry in motion'. Whether Angie's Aunt

Lucy has knobbly knees and skinny, scaly legs with curled up feet and pointed toe-nails I really couldn't say, since from the epiglottis downwards the minutiae of her anatomy had never been open to my inspection - a deprivation which, I must add, I do not blame for any shortcomings in my personal development. On reflection, I concluded that the appearance of Angie's Aunt Lucy was not a matter to be judged purely upon appearances.

'All my little tribe - I call them that you know,' the old lady had continued. (What tribe was this? Angie's Aunt Lucy, a cannibal? Such a revelation would surely push the Melton and Middlewick Messenger to new heights of sensationalism: *CANIBALISM IN CAMPERLEY - SPINSTER SPILLS THE BEINGS.*)

Angie's Aunt Lucy sipped her port and scrumpy and continued expansively, 'As I was saying, my little tribe are all would-be vegetarians. You know... strong vegetarian tendencies but, being seriously understaffed in the will power department, they yield to the slightest temptation.'

I found it all too confusing. Exactly where one chicken eating another chicken - albeit a vegetarian chicken - ranks in that grey area between the vegan and the out-and-out carnivore was well beyond my ken.

Anyway, back to the chicken crisis. Apparently, as dusk approached Angie's Aunt Lucy became anxious that the local foxes, themselves not conviction vegetarians, might find some way of luring the stricken chicken to a fate worse than – or in fact exactly equal to – death. So, having tucked her voluminous skirt up into her knickers, and looking more like a down-at-heel Elizabethan courtier than a middle-aged Shropshire spinster, the venerable old lady clambered into the alder tree, all the while clucking words of comfort to the frightened fowl.

As she admitted to us later, from the comfort of her hospital bed, 'Having shimmied as far along the branch as I dared, I found I was still an arm's length from my poor dear Susie. They all have names, of course, and during term time, at least, they come when I call them. But not Susie, not this time. She wouldn't budge. She just sat there shivering her wing feathers as if to say, "Please help me. I promise to be good if you'll save me."

'Well, I knew that branch was too thin further out to take my weight,' Angie's Aunt Lucy had continued, after cocking her head to the other side to equalise the wear on her sparse neck muscles. 'But the way I worked it out, if I could share my weight between *two* branches, that would halve the load on each, making it safe to shimmy further out over the pond. So I put one foot across to the next overhanging branch and...'

'But Aunt Lucy!' Angie interrupted her aunt, just when it was getting to what I thought was the really exciting bit. 'There's only one long branch hanging over the duck pond. I was there last week with the children, and-'

'Yes, dear. Precisely! And I do realise that now. But in the heat of the moment, let's just say I stepped off one branch into its reflection in the water below. Anyway, the result was quite stunning. I swivelled round onto my back and made a grab for my hat. That was a terrible error of judgement on my part. Whatever came over me, putting my hat before poor Susie's very life. Anyway, Susie and I parted company, her catapulting violently upwards and me gliding none too gently downwards. I recall shuddering in mid air at the thud of poor Susie's head against the trunk of the tree, and thinking, "now it's my turn". The next thing I remember is coming to with water lapping my nostrils. Thank goodness we'd had a drought! D'you know, the- Goodness gracious me!'

Angie's Aunt Lucy banged her hands against opposite sides of her head. If she's been doing that for sixty-odd years, I thought, maybe it's the bangs to the head rather than living for too long with too many chickens that's responsible for the unusual shape of her cranium.

'Oh! Goodness gracious me!' she repeated, in case we weren't listening the first time.

'Goodness gracious me, *what*?' I asked, anxiously.

'Goodness gracious this... Do you realise I could have walked into the duck pond and reached my Susie without all this to do. Then poor Dr Thomas wouldn't have gotten so awfully confused and upset.'

From discussions with various of the medical staff at Melton General, it appears that, once she had dragged herself out of the water, the most cursory inspection was enough to tell Angie's Aunt Lucy that all was very far from well. Apart from a huge swelling under her left armpit, which turned out to be Susie, a little dazed but otherwise none the worse for her travels, Angie's Aunt Lucy could see there was something else amiss: something was not quite right in her frontal region. She also had the good sense to realise that such a fall might have caused serious internal injuries. This was an emergency. So, tucking the soggy, dizzy hen back inside her jumper where it would soon dry out, Angie's Aunt Lucy had dialled 999 and asked to be taken to hospital straight away. But she had refused to lie down in the ambulance, insisting, instead, on sitting up and shouting helpful directions to the driver.

'Left at the end of the road. No, not here, silly! We haven't reached the start of the road yet: we're still in the lane. That's better, now left again about half a mile before you come to the post box. Well, Susie, dear, are you feeling better now?'

The ambulance swerved, almost toppling a bollard. The driver had turned round in time to see Angie's Aunt Lucy carefully lifting a live chicken, feet first, from the front of her jumper. For the rest of the journey the hen and its owner clucked away contentedly, leaving the ambulance driver to find his own way through the town centre.

As for letting the ambulance staff examine her, of that there was no chance. Only once in her life had Angie's Aunt Lucy ever called for medical attention, and this was it: she wanted to see a proper hospital doctor, a specialist. She would settle for nothing less. And it was only after the ambulance driver had solemnly promised to return Susie to the chicken pen at Camperley Cottage that Angie's Aunt Lucy had agreed to be stretchered from the ambulance.

For young Dr Thomas, the houseman who examined her in Casualty, Angie's Aunt Lucy was more co-operative. She even submitted to his request to strip off - up to a point. Well, actually, she refused to undress at all until a screen was brought and erected across one corner of the room, even though the only people in the room were the young doctor and herself. But she saw no reason to remove that final protective layer, her knickers and long-sleeved vest. Winter and summer they remained with her, waking and sleeping, save for a few minutes on bath night when they, too, could look forward to soap followed by a fortnight's rest in the linen cupboard while their deputies took over responsibility for providing cover.

'There's no blood, so there must be quite enough skin to go round. I take it you've seen enough skin not to need to see mine which, in any case, is working perfectly?' She peered intensely at the houseman who shuffled his feet and averted his gaze. His mouth opened and closed, but his mind sent it no words to work with.

Angie's Aunt Lucy felt she had been rather hard on the young man, and she continued in more helpful vein, 'I'm sure you'll find the problem, like beauty, is more than skin deep. I really don't think looking at my skin will help. Try again!'

The houseman looked again, touching the lump gingerly. Such a nasty swelling in the middle of the old lady's collar bone convinced him that this was, indeed, an emergency. Probably a compound fracture

- serious at any age. But then, there were other possibilities, of course. A growth, perhaps...

'Have you been to your GP for a check up lately, Mrs Winston?'

'I'm sorry, young man. You'll have to put it in layman's language for me. All this medical jargon goes way over my head, I'm afraid.'

He tried again, a quavering voice betraying a nervous disposition, 'Have you seen a doctor lately?'

'I thought you said you were a doctor.' Her eyes narrowed accusingly.

'Yes, but...'

'Ah! I see, but you want to obtain a second opinion. Well I'm afraid I wouldn't know how to arrange that, I don't know any other doctors. But surely you must know one or two?'

The question was rather unexpected, and the houseman did not respond. Instead, he took a second glance at the region of the swelling, held his chin and sucked air noisily through a gap between his front teeth. It was a technique he had learned from a pre-eminent specialist at St Mary's - guaranteed to give the impression you were carefully thinking through some difficult diagnosis and must under no circumstances be interrupted. It didn't work with Angie's Aunt Lucy.

'Like a hint?' She offered, politely.

'I... yes please.'

The houseman's next attack of indecision came at a most unfortunate time, and he failed to get in an emphatic 'not' before Angie's Aunt Lucy chipped in with, 'What about an X-ray?'

'What a good idea,' mumbled the houseman, near to tears, and he phoned for a porter.

As soon as the porter appeared Angie's Aunt Lucy disappeared, behind the screen. The porter was duly sent out, while the old lady eased herself into the wheelchair and the houseman covered her with blankets. Only then was the bemused porter allowed to proceed with his charge.

'Oh, David... er... would you tell Doris that it's OK for Mrs Winston to keep her underclothes on.'

Angie's Aunt Lucy was taken from X-ray straight to the Emergency Ward, where no amount of matronly persuasion would get her out of her undies and into a hospital nightie.

Meanwhile the houseman, having pored over the X-rays, began to have doubts about the value of his years of training. He could see there was a growth of some sort but a precise diagnosis was quite beyond him. He sought the advice of two senior colleagues, one a registrar who thought he had seen everything to which the human body could be host; neither had seen anything like it before.

It was with some trepidation that he approached the old lady lying contentedly in her hospital bed, obviously unaware of the advanced state of her disease. How best to break it to her? Exploratory surgery; that was the usual phrase. But would she understand? Ward Sister would know what's best.

'Er... Sister. It's Mrs Winston. I'm not sure how best to break it...'

But Angie's Aunt Lucy had sharp ears.

'It's OK doctor! It'll break all by itself, believe me. Couple of weeks tucked up cosy in here and The Ragged Old Cockerel will have something to cluck over.'

And with that she pulled down the top inch of her vest to reveal a speckled brown egg.

-ooOoo-

6 Hyphen

All that any of us remembered of Steven H Smythe was his prophecy. 'I don't just think, I *know*,' he had said, and we had all stopped laughing. It was so untypical, so unexpected. The laughter soon returned, but the prophecy had been printed indelibly on our memories. On mine anyway, and Jill and Angie say they remember it as clearly as if it was yesterday. The boys are less certain, but Peter ought to remember because he sat next to Steven on our first day at The Big School.

Steven hadn't been to nursery school with the rest of us, and so Elm Road Primary was his first taste of formal education. It seems he never really got over the shock of his mum leaving him alone with all us kids. On the first morning he had stood at the side of the playground staring pleadingly at her through the iron railings, and she had squinted back at him through her bottle-bottom spectacles until Miss Simmons herded us into the classroom.

Steven H Smythe was a loner, much more an observer of life than a participant. Hyphen-Smythe, we used to call him, or more often just plain Hyphen. Not that we knew what a hyphen was. You don't at that age, do you? And what the aitch stood for he never would say. But then I can't remember him saying very much at all. Except for that prophecy. At playtime he usually stayed in the classroom, and even when Miss Simmons shooed him out he just stood around waiting for the bell to call an end to our fun and games and his misery. It must be very sad to be so shy, but at the age of eight who thinks of things like that?

It was late spring, sunny but with a cool breeze. I wore my duffel coat with the hood that kept falling over my eyes. It had great big toggles, and I used to fiddle with them until they came loose and mum would have to sew them on again.

'I don't know!' mum would complain. 'Why can't they make clothes like they used to. It's a good job you didn't lose the toggle, Susan. I wouldn't know where to start looking for a new one.'

Duffel coats were all the rage in those days. They hardly made the most realistic of wedding dresses, but a regimented secondary education system had not yet stripped us of our imaginations and weddings were flavour of the month, at least with the girls. Angie was always the one for weddings, eagerly anticipating the splice of life even at that tender age. Anyway, after lunch which being working class kids, we always called dinner , Angie, Jill and I cornered Peter and Jim. We needed one more groom to complete the set. Most of the boys in our class were playing football, but Angie and Jill got hold of Hyphen and dragged him into the playground. He did not look at all happy - not that he said anything, but I could tell from his eyes. They glared with a resentment that seemed to be directed at me for not intervening. But I didn't, because I wanted to be in Angie's gang. All the girls did and some of the boys, but obviously not Hyphen. A couple of years later and the boys would run for miles rather than play anything as sissy as weddings.

Then, as now, Angie organised everything. She paired herself with Peter, Jill with Hyphen, and me with Jim.

'I'm not playing,' Hyphen blurted. 'You've got it all wrong. It should be Angie and Jim, and Jill with Peter. And I am going to marry Susan.'

Angie broke the stunned silence. 'It's my game, and I decide who marries who,' she snapped. 'It doesn't matter what you think, Hyphen Smythe!'

'I don't think, I *know*,' Steven had replied angrily. And with that he ran back into the classroom, leaving me to search for a new suitor.

I don't know how many times I have relived that moment - it must be dozens - feeling again the shame as Steven's eyes glared at me, his face all red and angry. I had never before seen him stare at anyone, his gaze being reserved almost exclusively for the ground just ahead of his feet. Was it anger, or was it embarrassment? Miss Simmons must have felt sorry for him, because she let him stay in the classroom until the bell rang. I never found a groom, so the wedding game was never played out.

And that's how things remained for nearly thirty years. I had plenty of friends, but nobody special. Nobody special enough to ask me to get spliced, that is. All through my late teens and twenties I was busy, what with mum's illness and then Mrs P next door. I didn't *have* to take Mrs P on, but she had nobody else and to be honest she was much more fun than the telly. And even when her voice went, she used to listen and nod. It was company. We invented our own sign language. I still miss her, the poor dear.

Steven never spoke to me again, nor as far as I know to any of the others, but he continued to stare. He stared at me through the classroom window when he was inside and I was out. I tried not to stare back, but you know how difficult it is. A year later he had to leave our school because his folks moved up north somewhere to run a sub post office. That was it. The staring – the being stared at, that is – stopped and I thought no more about it.

I might have guessed which of us would marry first. At Jim and Angie's wedding reception Jill made a joke of it: 'What about that weird boy? Steven with a vee... remember? Steven H Smythe. "I don't think, I *know*."' Jill mimicked his wavering voice so well, and we all laughed.

'Well, who knows?' Jill said with a childish chuckle, 'Perhaps he did know. Anyway, I wonder who'll be next.'

We laughed about it all over again when Jill got married... not to Peter, but to Johnny Shepherd, her teenage sweetheart from next door. A foregone conclusion, really, and not something Steven could ever have known about. But nothing could have prepared us for the news of the honeymoon disaster.

Apparently they were on a coastal footpath and Johnny was taking photographs of Jill. She was looking into the sun as he stepped back to frame the shot. She watched as Johnny's silhouette disappeared over the edge of the cliff. A fisherman found his body a week later washed up into a rocky cove. Some people said Jill was still in shock when she married Peter only eight months later. It certainly made me wonder yet again about Hyphen's prophecy.

'Don't be so wet!' Peter chided. 'Coincidence, that's all. He probably went around saying things like that to loads of kids. We only remember because... well, because some of what he said has come true. Make enough prophesies and some of them are bound to come true. In any case, what came true is only true because we made it happen. We wanted it to.'

'And what about you, Susan?' Angie asked. 'What do you want to happen? Are you planning on putting an ad in the lost and found column? Missing, one small red hyphen. Hey... does anybody remember what the aitch was for?'

'Havelock-Smythe,' I told her. I had found out from Miss Simmons when she came to Mrs P's funeral. 'But don't you worry Angie, I'm firmly glued to the shelf. Far too set in my ways to share what's left of my life with anyone. Anyway, who would want me, especially now?'

I shut up, and was greatly relieved when Angie changed the subject. Wedding receptions have always made me feel... well, not sad exactly, but uneasy somehow.

~~~

It came as quite a shock when Stan asked me out to the theatre. If I hadn't been struck dumb I might have said no, but he took my silence for agreement and said, 'Okay then. We can go straight from work.

Grab a bite on the way. There should just be time.' I had to sneak out from the office at lunchtime to buy something to wear.

Stan Hardy had joined the department a week earlier as a clerical officer. His desk was opposite mine. Whenever I looked up from my work, there was Stan, shy, quiet, eyes down and working hard. I guess most people would describe him as ordinary. Boring even. So what? Probably that's how they see me, too. I'll spare you the details; suffice it to say that Stan and I got on. We got on well enough to get engaged three months later. As Stan said, at our age we couldn't afford to waste time. That's why we settled for a quiet wedding near his folks' place in Sunderland. They are quiet, gentle people too, just like Stan. I met them for the first time at the registry office.

We were there far too early, Stan and me. It wasn't raining, so we had walked. Separate taxis seemed silly when we were coming from a hotel just one street away.

A little old lady wearing bottle-bottom spectacles poked her head round the office door, smiled at me and said, 'The senior registrar will see you in a few moments.'

Stan's folks were next to arrive. We hugged as though we hadn't seen one another for years, even though we had all had breakfast together less than an hour ago. Then, just in time, my gang turned up, and in force: Angie, Jim, Jill and Peter. You should have seen their faces when the little old lady poked her head round the door again and gave me another beaming smile.

'Please come through, Susan,' she said. 'Mr Havelock-Smythe will marry you now.'

-oo0oo-

7   In the Fullness of Time

Peter Miller sighed wearily. 'I know you're upset, Jen, but we'll just have to leave it 'till morning. It's hopeless in this light. The more we trample about, the harder it'll be to find the blasted thing tomorrow.'

'Oh, really?' Jenny Miller retorted. 'Well it might be just a blasted thing to you, Peter, but a wedding ring's supposed to mean something...'

'Oh, I'm sorry, Jenny. Really I am. It's just that... well, I know you. Once you get into a state, you lie awake all night. Next day you're fit for nothing. That's not going to help, now is it? A ring can't dissolve. It won't go anywhere, so we're bound to find it eventually. The best thing we can do is to leave something as a marker. Tomorrow, in the daylight, we'll find it easily enough. You'll see.'

Jenny smiled, and pushed back an errant wisp of auburn hair. Reason was on his side, of course. It usually was. He was the logical planner, she the irrational dreamer.

'Promise, then? First thing after breakfast?'

'No! Before breakfast. And I won't start on anything else until we find it. If need be I'll go over the whole garden with a sieve. Anyway, it'll be an opportunity to clear away some of the rubbish.'

They linked arms and headed indoors. 'One good thing, the weather's on our side,' Peter continued. 'I know there's loads to keep us busy inside, but if it stays half decent we really ought to make the most of it. The whole garden needs doing, before the weeds take over completely. So cheer up, Jenny love. Everything is going to be okay. We'll find your ring tomorrow, you'll see. Come on, let's have supper.'

The Millers spent the whole of the following morning digging and sifting, starting from the cane that marked the spot where Jenny had taken off her ring and gradually extending the search until they had cleared a wide strip on either side of the path leading from the lane to their front door. They unearthed a handful of coins, a couple of torch batteries and an old watch. They did not find the ring.

'I'll bet a magpie has taken it,' Jenny said woefully during a brief rest from the backbreaking toil. 'They do that sort of thing, you know. Remember the one we saw in the lane yesterday. One for sorrow!' She rubbed her finger where the ring had been for so many years. The swelling's going down, that's one good thing. It's still pretty sore, though. Perhaps I should have left it on. Maybe the ring saved my finger from being crushed. I hadn't thought of that, Peter.'

Her husband looked up but made no reply.

'I was thinking,' she went on. 'Last night, while you were fast asleep. It'll be twenty-seven years this July, and until last night that ring hadn't been off my finger since the day you put it on. Not even when I had David. They wanted me to, you know, but I wouldn't. I said it was stuck.' She chuckled, with a wicked grin that faded in an instant as she added: 'D'you think what happened yesterday was some sort of message? A warning, maybe, about this place or something?'

'Now don't start all that again, Jen, please. You chose this place, remember. All right,' he added hurriedly, 'buying The Brambles was a joint decision. But nobody pushed you into it. And squashing your finger in the wardrobe door was your own fault, too. I said don't try to move any of the big things until I'd finished with the tea chests. You really can be the most stubborn... Well, enough said. But if it'll make you feel any better, as soon as we've finished unloading the van I'll run you into town and we can get another ring, just...'

Too late, Peter Miller realised he had made a serious tactical error. He held up both hands in submission as his wife stormed at him.

'Oh, no you don't. That's just typical of you...'

'Whoa! Hang on, Jenny, and just listen a moment before you snap at me. I hadn't finished. I was going to say *just for now*. I'll ask David to bring his metal detector at the weekend. It's not so far for him to come, now. And in any case, I bet you can't wait to show him round.'

'Oh Peter! You're a genius...' But the delight on her face soon faded as an old spectre loomed before her once more. She continued in more subdued tone, 'But that won't help if a magpie *has* taken it, will it?'

'Well at least we'll know one way or the other, Jen.'

'All right, but I'm not having another ring. It's my own ring or no ring at all. And that's final. So why don't you clear up this mess and I'll fix us a snack? Sandwich okay? Then if you like we can pop into town for a meal this evening. But no jewellers' shops. Understood?'

Jenny Miller scanned the devastation resulting from the morning's excavation, hoping that by some chance the mid-day sun might glint from a facet of the gold ring. But it had worn thin, with most of the patterning long gone. She turned away, tears near the surface again, and wondered why the loss hurt so much. She still had Peter, and at last they would have time together. That was the main thing. She knew that early retirement carried penalties - financially things would be tight, even with a much smaller place - but Peter was right: moving had been her idea, and really it was she who had pressed *him*. He could have stayed on another two years at Witherby's – in fact Old Man Witherby himself had virtually begged him to stay. But the past twelve months had been pretty grim, what with the reorganisation and the continual cut-backs. Everyone watching everyone else, Peter had said. Watching and waiting for someone to make a mistake; only doing things to avoid blame; nothing positive to look forward to. He had found it all pretty depressing. Then young David had got his promotion and a transfer to head office, and that had been the clincher. David on his own two feet at last, independent and about as secure as anyone in employment could be nowadays. They had said the headquarters job would be for three years and then he could apply for a vacancy nearer home, but Jenny knew her son only too well: if an assistant manager post came up he'd jump for it even if it was in the middle of nowhere. So ambitious - not at all like his father! Peter would never have...

Jenny was roused from her daydreaming by a call.

'Okay! Coming...' she replied, wondering what he could possibly be doing upstairs. But he obviously needed her help, so she rinsed her hands and began the climb. When she was halfway up, he called again, this time from the lounge.

'Is that lunch ready yet, Jen? I'm famished.'

'Look, I can't be in two places at once. If you want me to help you upstairs, fine. But you might at least let me know if you can't be bothered to wait. Don't expect me to traipse about after you all day.'

Peter frowned. Jenny's patience needed regular feeding. In fact, he had to admit, they both got a bit snappy if meals were delayed. And this week just about every meal had been late. Or cancelled.

'I didn't tell you to go walkabouts! I've been trying to make some sort of sense of your weird labelling system. Just what, for example, does 'P-Cl' mean?'

'It means Peter's clothes, you idiot,' she retorted. 'I haven't got time to waste writing everything in longhand. It's cryptic because it's meant to be cryptic. It means leave it to me, I'll unpack it when the wardrobe's ready. I thought maybe that was what you were doing upstairs.'

'Jenny! For the last time, I wasn't up there. You don't honestly think I can just hoist a double wardrobe on my shoulders and march upstairs with it, do you? It'll have to stay down here until David can give us a hand.'

'Well, if you weren't upstairs, who called me?'

'Jenny, love, I only asked if lunch was ready. Would I go upstairs to ask you that when I know you're in the kitchen? Well... would I?'

'Peter! You're not listening. I said someone called from upstairs. Go and check... now!'

Peter Miller knew the score. Jenny could hardly be described as the nervous type, but when she got wound up she got well and truly wound up. And something had got to her now, so check he would.

And check he did – thoroughly - and he found nothing unusual, but he knew better than to tease his wife when she was upset. This business of the ring was really getting to her. Silly, really, but he too felt the loss far more than he could explain. Things - things you just own but can't do anything with, that is - had never meant much to him. Nor to Jenny, really. That was the odd thing about it. And they hardly ever raised voices to one another, but since the accident last night they had barely exchanged a comforting word.

'There's absolutely nothing there, darling. Maybe it was the wind. Or a creaking hinge. I don't think this old house has any of the other sort.'

What?'

'Hinges, Jenny dear. We've only got the creaky sort. That's what I was looking for in the lounge.'

'Then there's something very wrong with your priorities, Peter, if all you can think about is changing door hinges. What we need right now is...'

'Oil, you clot!' he laughed. 'I was looking for the tea chest where we put the oil can and such stuff. For the hinges. Oiling hinges is a lot easier than changing them.'

'All right, there's no need to be sarcastic. The penny's dropped, thank you.'

Jenny Miller grinned and pushed her husband back into the armchair just as he was struggling to rise. Peter grabbed her apron and pulled her onto his lap.

'Really! And I thought you'd retired. Don't tell me that only means from work.'

He kissed her neck, pinched her bottom and chided, 'Never go to bed on an empty stomach. That's what Great Aunt Agatha always said. An' she were never wrong, or so she would have it. So get thee gone into that there kitchen, me deerio, an' let's see what you can do to keep yer ole man alive a bit longer.'

Jenny couldn't help laughing, no matter how many times she heard his silly nonsense.

"Shurrup, ya silly ole eejut", she would sometimes retort. But that only seemed to encourage him and he'd keep on all the more. Instead she replied, 'Okay, darling. Take a couple of folding chairs out onto the lawn, and I'll bring lunch out on a tray. It would be a shame to be indoors with the weather so good.'

The garden chairs had been packed away in pairs, their canvas seats protected by thick cardboard. By the time Peter had undone the string and sticky tape Jenny was beckoning to him. He waved and called out, 'Coming!'

Outside, he found an area of reasonably level pasture - what the estate agent had imaginatively described as lawn - and sited the chairs facing the sun. He looked about but his wife was nowhere to be seen. *Now* where had she gone? Peter Miller walked right around the house but saw no sign of her. He knew this game! She was running round ahead of him. Quickly reversing direction, he made another rapid circuit of the house, but caught not a glimpse of her.

'Hey! What's the idea, Jen. You trying to lose a stone or two before lunch?'

Just then Jenny Miller emerged from the front door with a tray of sandwiches and cold drinks. 'Patience is a virtue,' she reminded him. 'I've only got one pair of hands. If you think...' The puzzled look on her husband's face cut her short. 'What's wrong, Peter. You look as if you've just seen a...'

'You were here... a minute ago... weren't you, Jen? Here, in the garden, I mean.'

'Course not! Not a minute ago, no. Earlier, yes, with you, looking for the ring. But not since. Why? Was there somebody out here?'

Peter Miller's frown deepened. 'Yes. I mean, I think so, but...'

'But what?' she asked.

'Well... I saw someone all right. No, not here. Over there on the path, where we were digging. I could have sworn it was you, Jen. For a moment I thought you were still looking for the ring. Then you... I mean she... waved. Like this... as if to say "come and help" or something.'

'Peter! Stop it! You're frightening me. If this is your idea of a joke, it's not funny.'

'No, Jen, there was someone. A woman. Definitely. I thought it was you, but... she was older, much older.' He thought for a moment, and then exclaimed, 'The blasted cheek of it! I know this place has been empty for months, but if people think they can just barge into our garden and go mooching around... Well, the sooner we let it be known that The Brambles has got new owners the better.'

'You probably frightened her more than she did you, darling. Have your lunch now.'

'I wasn't frightened. It'd take more than a batty old bag poking about in the petunias to frighten me. Anyway, she soon hopped it. It's lucky for her that she did, or...'

'All right! Calm down. Anyway, there aren't any petunias. Nor anything else apart from dandelions, ground elder and couch grass.'

They ate their sandwiches in silence, and the peace of the spring countryside crowded in on them, pushing away any worries. In no time Peter Miller's thoughts drifted along pleasanter lines: his plans for the house, the workshop, the garden, and maybe a greenhouse. Time was theirs now. No rushing for the seven fifteen, five days a week, and spending most of the weekend in semi-convalescence ready for another bruising five days... and another... another... another. He felt his head roll, and shook himself awake. Jenny had gone - the tray also, although the glass of orange squash was still in his hand.

'Better shift,' he muttered to himself. 'There's a lot to do!'

The promise of the morning had been broken, and high cloud had brought a hint of drizzle with the threat of much worse to come. Not to worry, he thought, it was still only April. The best was yet to come, and they'd be able to enjoy it, together. All those things they used to do before they had David, careers, a mortgage. But at least they had seen the light before it was too late. Not like poor old Mike and Elsie...

'I'm up here. In the front bedroom,' Jenny Miller called down to her husband. 'What do you want?' From down below the anxious calls continued. He's going deaf. I'll swear he is, she thought.

Jenny crossed to the bathroom and eased open the casement. She looked out across the lawn. There was no sign of her husband, but at the side of the house there certainly was activity. The sound was unmistakable: someone was digging in the garden. Peter must still be trying to find her ring. Then, through the opaque casement - why have textured glass when there were no neighbours? - Jenny saw the patterns of light and shade altering. In the garden below, someone was moving. She swung the window right back. There he was, his back towards her bent low over the fork, the waxed cotton jacket looking much the worse for wear. And that ridiculous hat - where on earth had that come from! No, it wasn't a hat - it was his hair, all white and fluffy. There he was, down on all fours on the damp soil, waving and calling excitedly: 'Jenny! Look! After all this time... look!'

All at once, Peter Miller felt uneasy. The water was still running in the bathroom, and Jenny had been in there an age. Something was wrong. He had to go to her.

Mounting the stairs two at a time he burst into the bathroom, sliding to a halt behind her. Jenny didn't turn round, didn't say a word. She just stood there, staring down into the garden. Peter turned off the tap and eased himself alongside her.

'What is it, Jen? What's the matter?'

'You've found it! Oh, Peter! After all these years, you've found it!' Her voice sounded distant and somehow strange.

Jenny could see what Peter could not. She saw an old woman clutching something to her breast, something very small, very precious. Then the white-haired old man put his arms around her, as if sharing her joy. For a while the old couple just stood, arms around each another, very still.

Tears welled up in Jenny Miller's eyes, and the old couple faded into the mist. Jenny blinked and wiped away her tears. The scene came into focus: the gate, the path, the empty seed beds, nothing more. Peter held her tight.

'Jenny, love, don't cry. I do care, really I do. I haven't found it yet, but I'll keep on looking until I do. That's a promise, sweetheart.'

She squeezed his hand. 'I know, darling. And I'm quite sure you'll find it... in the fullness of time.'

-ooOoo-

8   Contrariwise

The consultant's door opened and a young nurse poked his head out. As one, the line of patients seated against one wall of the corridor lifted their heads from the screens of their smart phones, which had at last made out-of-date celebrity magazines redundant. They braced themselves for the call to Consulting Room 1. There was only one consulting room, but all rooms in the hospital were numbered. Perhaps an administrator with a small but expansionist mind had decreed there should be no exceptions.

'Mrs Johnson?'

Two smartly-dressed thirty-somethings, one blonde the other brunette seated three places apart, stood up and took a step forward. In unison they stepped back and looked around uncertainly.

'Mrs Emily Johnson?' The nurse swept his gaze between the two candidates and tried to smother a grin.

'That's me,' the blond woman said, stepping forward again.

'Sorry,' the other Mrs Johnson said. 'I'm Barbara. I don't mean I'm sorry I'm Barbara. Oh, and I didn't mean to imply I'm not sorry I'm not you.'

The other Mrs Johnson, Emily Johnson, laughed and said, 'It's okay, really. Anyway, I might be sorry I'm me, depending on what shows up on my scan.'

'Good luck,' Barbara Johnson said, returning to her seat more amused than embarrassed. Over the years, her garrulousness had made her more friends than enemies. And if people were going to take a dislike to her it's best they do so from the start. Some people did read her initial chattiness as showing off, even arrogance. They were wrong, Barbara knew. It was just her way of coping with being with people she didn't know. She always assumed that other people were smarter, better educated, more interesting than she was. But she got on well with most people, once she got to know them, and actually she did a lot more listening and thinking than talking.

Barbara wondered what kind of scan Emily Johnson could be having to be so worried about the results. Her own consultation was routine and she'd hardly given it a second thought after putting the appointment into her diary. Over the past four years her six-monthly blood tests and scans had all shown no sign of the tumour returning. The surgery had been minimally invasive, thanks to dear old Dr Wilson spotting the early signs, and now the physical scar was equally unobtrusive. The checkups were important, she knew, but in between she just got on with life.

The door to Consulting Room 1 opened and Emily Johnson emerged, chatting with the nurse as together they set off down the corridor towards Reception. Suddenly Emily stopped, turned back and approached Barbara Johnson. 'All clear,' she said. 'And thanks for the good luck message. It seems to have worked!'

Barbara beamed. 'I'm really pleased for you,' she said. Emily smiled and set off after the nurse, who was ostentatiously holding open the swing door open for his patient.

'Mrs Barbara Johnson?'

Barbara went in to the consultation room, and the other queueing patients turned their heads back to the phone screens that few of them were actually reading.

Fifteen minutes later, after getting another all clear report and advice on exercises that might improve the mobility of her left shoulder, Barbara set off to complete the *How-did-we-do-today?* form that the receptionist seemed to treat very much like a prison's *Discharge-on-Parole* document.

'Hi Barbara! How did it go?' It was Emily who, having been awarded a pass grade for her discharge paper by the receptionist, had decided to hover until her namesake emerged.

'Fine. I'm perfectly fine, thanks Emily.'

'I just wondered... d'you fancy a coffee? There's a new Starbucks on the other side of town. It's where Bon Marché used to be.'

'That would be nice.' Barbara had nothing planned for the rest of the afternoon, and Dave was away on his weekly three-day tour of northern clients, so this was one of the four evenings when she ate alone, either at home or in Chelini's, the only restaurant within walking distance of her home.

'You came here by car?' Emily asked.

Barbara nodded.

'Follow me. Mine's the red Clio over there.' Emily gestured towards the tree-lined edge of the hospital car park.

~~~

Seated at a table by the window, the two Mrs Johnsons sipped their cappuccinos. They had resisted the temptation of biscottis, cookies and madeleines, although each secretly thought that had they been alone they might well have succumbed.

'This is nice,' Emily said. 'I'm really glad we bumped into one another. Do you... Oh no, I'm not going to ask you the corny old question my husband picked me up with. Tell me, though... what do you do, Barbara? For a living, I mean. When you're not having scans, that is.'

'I'm a pharmacist, Barbara replied. 'I've just started a new job in Boots near where I live, in Grafton Swinsbury. How about you?'

'Oh, nothing very clever. I'm just a teaching assistant at our local junior school in Sharpstone. D'you know it?' Barbara shook her head. 'The village is tucked away just off the Markham road, about ten miles from here. It's a nice little community and I like the work, and most of the kids. Even some of the teachers.'

They both laughed. 'Only kidding!' Emily added, spilling some of her coffee. 'Oops... that's typical me. iIf only I'd given in to temptation I could have mopped it up with a biscotti.'

'True,' Barbara replied. 'Sadly, there are just as many calories in one tall cappuccino as there are in a packet of those delicious biscottis – assuming Dave's right about that.'

'Dave? Is that your husband?'

Barbara nodded. 'Yes. Well, he's Peter David Johnson, actually, but his dad was Pete so he got called by his second name. He prefers it to Pete, and to be honest so do I.'

Emily shook her head in amazement. 'You're not going to believe this, Barbara... my husband's a Dave, too. Just the one first name. His parents had six kids and so they went sparing with the Christian names. Dai, we all call him. He's Welsh. Not that you'd guess to hear him talk. He was born in Swansea, but his family left Wales when he was only three, so he can't remember any of it. His folks called him Dai, and it's just stuck.'

'What does your husband do?' Barbara asked.

'He's what used to be called a travelling salesman. When we first got married he covered the south west of England and could get home every night. Then, in the last recession, the company got rid of half their sales staff and Dai drew the short straw. But he says all the straws were short. Dai kept the south west but now has to cover the north west as well, seeing each client once a fortnight instead of every week. A London-based woman looks after her old patch and has also had to take on the north east. What it means is that all the reps now spend days on end away from home. The one I feel most sorry for is the Northern Ireland guy. He now has to cover Wales and Scotland as well. Dai says he's a young chap, unattached, and doesn't seem to mind too much.'

For several seconds after Emily had stopped talking, Barbara sat stony faced, saying nothing, her cup half way to her lips. Then she put the cup down so quickly that it hit the table with an attention-grabbing crash.

'What is it, Barbara? Are you okay? Is it something I said?'

'No... I mean... It's something I could have said. Should have. About *my* Dave. He's a van man, too. His firm makes and distributes counter displays for chemists' shops. So I guess you can work out how Dave and I met.'

It was Emily's turn to be stuck for words. She stared at her feet and frowned.

'I know what you're thinking,' Barbara said. 'But it can't be. My Dave wouldn't do that. He just wouldn't. He texts me every morning and evening when he's away, and he phones from the van if he's on the road during my lunch break.'

Emily had recovered her composure. 'I'm sure you're right. Dai and me, we're solid too. No kids. Just the two of us. Separate hobbies – he's into golf and DIY, but I'm the one who does the cooking and gardening. We're both happy that way. But we're Emily-and-Dai, like it's just one word. An item, to everyone we know. It's just that... it's such an incredible coincidence, all of it. Two Mrs Johnson's waiting to see the same consultant. Both of us married to delivery man David Johnson, covering the same area but out of sync.'

'Yes, truly weird. It's changeover day for us,' Barbara explained. 'Dave will be back in a couple of hours and I always do something special for dinner.'

Emily thought of asking what kind of food Dave liked best, but the question got stuck somewhere between brain and tongue. She tried again, 'What are–'

Barbara Johnson's iPhone buzzed and began sliding across the table. She picked it up, smiled at Emily and said, 'Sorry.' It wasn't a number she recognised. 'Hello?'... Yes... Barbara, yes.' As she listed a look of horror crept across her face, and her hands began to tremble. 'Yes, I'm about ten minutes away. Please tell him I'm on the way.' She stood up and said, 'It's Dave. He's crashed his van. He's been taken to Penmore Hospital. I've got to go.'

'Would you like me to drive you there,' Emily asked. 'That way, if there's anything you and Dave need I could fetch it for you.'

The two new friends rushed out to Emily's car and set off towards Penmore.

'Did they say how he was?' Emily asked as she sped at sixty through a forty limit.

'No. But he must be bad or he would have insisted on speaking to me. I'm really worried that-'

Barbara was cut short by another phone call, this time on Emily's phone, which was Bluetooth enabled and connected to her hands-free earpiece.

'Hello. Yes, I'm Emily... that's right. Why? What's wrong? Oh my God! Yes. About five minutes.' She glanced briefly at Barbara. 'Dai's had an accident in his van. That was the hospital.'

~~~

The door to Emergency Ward 1 opened and a nurse poked her head out. As one, the line of patients seated in the corridor lifted their heads from the screens of their smartphones, which had at last made out-of-date celebrity magazines redundant, and braced themselves for the call.

'Mrs Johnson?'

Two smartly-dressed thirty-somethings, one blonde the other brunette seated together stood up and took a step forward. The nurse checked her clipboard. 'Oh, er...'

'That's us,' the two Mrs Johnsons replied as one.

'Barbara?' The nurse hesitated. 'Your husband, Peter David Johnson, has a broken leg. He is in side ward A. The doctor is just checking on him one more time, and then I think you'll be able to take him home. And Emily... your husband is recovering from concussion. He is in side ward B. We'll have to do a few more tests, but we think David will get the okay to go home shortly. The ambulance staff said they were both very lucky. Not many people escape so lightly from a head-on collision.'

Emily looked at Barbara and said, 'I'm so glad we bumped into one another.'

'Me too,' Barbara said. 'I'm not so sure Dai and Dave will be feeling likewise.'

-oo0oo-

9 Pier Pressure

Lord Quarrello of Bickerton kicked the stuffed cat that he had bought to replace the aged moggie that had departed a year ago. He lived alone, no wife to harangue him: Lady Prunella had left him a year ago, taking the car, the cat and most of the vestiges of his inherited wealth. He had no need of the battered old Bentley, and he hated animals almost as much as he despised those wrinkled old vegetables in the House of Lords: snivelling clots, talking a load of bloody rot as they themselves rot on their blood-red benches. But he missed his wife. Without her, the crumbling old house had become even more of a mess. Meals were junk, and anything that broke stayed broken. But most of all he missed her as a target for his critical tirades. And so far he had failed to find a substitute.

Today the old peer would visit an even older pier. The pier must be a magnet for people, he thought, and it's no more than a ten minute walk away. Maybe there he would meet a worthy adversary, someone to bring meaning back to his life.

In his crumpled white-linen suit, straw Panama hat and tan deck shoes, Lord Quarrello set off for the promenade. Upon reaching the prom he turned west, and with the sun on his back he headed for the pier. It was too early for most of the tourists, who were still breakfasting in the hotels, B&Bs and guest houses that bordered the long sweeping curve of the promenade. A few sentinel souls sauntered slowly towards the pier entrance, chatting inconsequentially in the summer sunshine. None looked worthy of a jibe, Quarrello concluded, but he strode onwards, hopeful of conflict to come.

A small knot of assorted couples blocked the way to the pierhead, beguiled by a beckoning bearded manikin in a Perspex kiosk.

'Hey! Come on over, and let Zoltar show you your fortune.'

A young woman was jostled forward, but she stepped back quickly. 'Oh, no way! Not me. How about you, Carl? Or you, Tracey?'

'Come on over,' Zoltar urged.

'Go on then,' said Lord Quarrello, 'if you're stupid and gullible enough to waste your money on the manikin's meaningless mumblings. But I warm you... it will cost you an arm and a leg, and for what? Absolute drivel! Only idiots are taken in by this shoddy scam. Those with brains move on and make way for other duller dolts to line this charlatan's grubby pockets.'

As one, the group shuffled uneasily and then set off in silence towards the distant pierhead.

'Not as stupid as they looked, eh?' Lord Quarrello chuckled, gloating over his triumph at Zoltar's expense.

'Why you do that to me?' Zoltar asked. 'All I do is try to make a living by bringing a bit of joy into people's lives. Charm without harm... that's me.'

'You're just a pointless parasite,' Lord Quarrello retorted. 'The world has no need of your sort.'

Zoltar shrugged, or at least he would have if he could have. 'And does anyone need *you*?' he replied. 'I don't think so. For what it's worth I think you are a mean and miserable old man whose only aim in life is to spread conflict and gloom wherever you go. Well, don't do it here on this pier.'

'Huh! What you think is no skin off my nose.'

'You think so? You could be wrong about that,' Zoltar replied calmly.

'Why would anyone take notice of a turban-topped stuffed jacket in a plastic box? You should learn to show some respect. I am a peer of the realm.'

'That's as may be,' Zoltar replied. 'By this pier is my realm, and you are no longer welcome here.'

'*Your* pier, is it? Well, in that case if it was on fire I definitely wouldn't lift a finger to help you.'

'Then you will not be able to lift a finger to help yourself either,' Zoltar asserted, staring straight ahead. Lord Quarrello stared back at the manikin defiantly, until his nose began to itch and he couldn't avoid blinking. Fumbling for a handkerchief, he set off up the pier. 'Pathetic, yes; but prophetic? Not even slightly.'

Zoltar ignored the jibe and issued a welcome to the next little huddle of holidaymakers. 'Come on over...'

At the end of the pier, Lord Quarrello of Bickerton settled himself on one of the commemorative benches overlooking the fishing platform. *'In memory of Harold and Ivy Parsons of Shrewsbury, who loved this spot.'* Stupid thing to say. Only dimwits love spots, pimples, pustules. If they'd been here now he would have told them as much. But he was sitting there alone, watching as a trio of fisherman baited up their rods and cast out into the calm waters of the bay. On previous visits he had usually watched for ten minutes or so while the fishermen caught nothing, but today Lord Quarello watched them catch nothing for nearly half an hour, while a seagull and three oystercatchers scavenged for discarded bait morsels on the fishing platform, even stepping on the boots of one dozing angler.

'Stupid idiot,' Lord Quarello called out. 'Sitting there waiting for the bell on your rod tip to ring and tell you when it's done your fishing for you. It ain't gonna happen, I can promise you that much,' he prophesied.

Unruffled, the fisherman called back, 'No worries, man.'

No chance of a decent argument here, Lord Quarrello told himself. He sighed and sat back. Then a glint of sunlight caught his eye. It had reflected from something on the decking near his feet. Leaned forward, he saw a fingernail lying on the wooden planking. And then, as he watched, another landed beside it. When he tried to pick one of them up it fell from his grasp and dropped through a gap between the planking. He watched in fascination as the fingernail drifted on the breeze until a seagull plucked it from just above the surface of the sea. He tried again with the second nail, and yet again he failed.

Lord Quarrello stared at his fingers. Where there should have been flesh, skin and fingernails he saw only bones and sinews. Shuddering, he looked up at the sun, shook his head and lurched to his feet. Sunstroke... it must be that. He had to move into the shade, take a long cold drink, and get his head down until it cleared. But most of all he needed calamine lotion for his itching nose. He reached up to scratch the itch and heard the scrape of bone on bone.

Shunning the queue at the ice cream and cold drinks booth, the panicking peer hurtled back down the pier as fast as his old legs would take him, pushing brusquely past the group he had earlier snatched from Zoltar's clutches.

People in fancy-dress costumes were gathering beside the bouncy castle. 'Mum, dad... look at that old man,' a youngster in a White Rabbit outfit yelled. 'He's dressed as a skelington. That's not fair! What's a skelington got to do with Alice in Wonderland? Hey mister... you're cheating!'

But Lord Quarrello careered on regardless.

'Hey, don't come on over ever again,' Zoltar called, as a skeletal figure hurtled towards him.

'Get stuffed,' the peer retorted, pausing a pace beyond Zoltar's kiosk. 'Ah, but of course... that's all you are. A stuffed dummy. You can't fool me with your fuzzy forecasts and gormless gimmicks.'

And when Lord Quarrello pointed an accusing finger at Zoltar he saw fleshy skin, not mere bone and sinew. His head had cleared, the itching had stopped. He laughed defiantly, stepping forward and raising his fist in front of the manikin.

Immediately three more fingernails fluttered to the deck and were blown into the sea by a gust of wind. The hand, now entirely skeletal, flopped limply to Lord Quarrello's side. He stepped back and stared in horror as the flesh and skin slowly returned.

But he had lost all of his fingernails.

'Come on over and let Zoltar show you your fortune. But I warn you... try that again and it really *will* cost you an arm and a leg.'

-oo0oo-

10 Star Turn

'Was it worth it?' Salvorin asked. 'We're all 750 million years older, but are we any wiser than when we left planet Earth?'

Her two companions frowned, thought about it and came to the same conclusion.

'Probably not,' Gerou said for both of them. 'But having been in suspended animation for so very long we should at least give it a try rather than giving up. The system says this is the most Earth-like planet in the Canis Minor galaxy, and the system has had more than enough time to assess every single one of the planets in this tiny galaxy of barely a billion stars.

'Earth-like... and is that really the key criterion?' Belencu asked. His two companions laughed.

'Like planet Earth as humans found it, or Earth as we left it?' Salvorin asked of no one in particular. 'After a journey of 25,000 light years in this decrepit old system ship, that's the only question that really matters'.

'There's only one way to find out,' Belencu said. 'Let's go.'

After a journey of 25,000 light years plus an hour, the three surviving earthlings had their answer.

'We have travelled the universe in search of a planet that could support human life. At last we have found one... only to learn that its humans have done to it what we did to ours. This once lovely planet can no longer support life. We can't stay here, and there's no turning back, so we have to move on.'

'To where?' Gerou asked.

'It's your turn to choose a star, Salvorin,' Belencou said.

Salvorin nodded thoughtfully. 'A star somewhere else,' she said. 'We've just enough fuel left for one final blast. But first we need to make a crucial adjustment to the system's search criteria. We need the system ship to take us to a planet that can support all of planet Earth's life forms *except* humanity.'

'An excellent plan,' Gerou said. 'That sounds like a planet to die for.'

'Exactly,' Salvorin replied.

-ooOoo-

11 Flight of Fancy

'There was a loud bang,' the old lady said. 'It made me jump, and I spilt the tea I had been drinking.'

The highlight of the twins' week was when their parents took them to visit Aunt Sandra. Mum would take over auntie's kitchen and make them all a special Sunday dinner, and if she didn't need dad's help in the kitchen he either did repairs on the old house or worked in auntie's garden.

Sandra Quinn was actually Geraldine and Thomas's great aunt, and to nine-year-old Thomas Carrol she was by far the greatest aunt in the whole world. She wrote exciting adventure stories, and most weekends she would read one to the twins. Today Geraldine was practising her serve, hitting a tennis ball against the garden wall where the faded outline of a painted-on net was still just visible. Auntie Sandra had said it had been her father's idea when she was a little girl with no brothers or sisters to practice with. Later a proper tennis court had been put up at the end of the orchard, but that, his aunt had told them, was only when she had earned enough money to pay for it herself.

'I looked out and saw smoke and flames pouring from two of the four engines,' Sandra continued, 'and then the plane veered sharply to port.'

Thomas was having this story all to himself. He would tell Geraldine all about it tomorrow on the way back home.

'Veered to port means it swerved to the left, Thomas. Port and starboard were originally nautical terms, meaning left and right, but they are used in aviation too.'

The boy nodded. 'Port left, starboard right. Yes, okay. So then what happened?'

'The first officer, who had just left the flight deck and was walking down the cabin to stretch his legs, was thrown off balance. His head crashed against the side of a seat, and he was knocked unconscious. Blood was pouring from his forehead, and the senior air hostess rushed to help him. 'Go and make sure Tim's all right,' she yelled to her younger colleague, a trainee air hostess.'

The old lady glanced at the youngster. He was staring out at the sky, his eyes and mouth wide open. She smiled and went on, 'As the young air hostess entered the flight deck another of the engines spluttered, the nose tilted downwards and the plane began losing height. With a loud crash, the door between the flight deck and the cabin slammed shut, knocking the air hostess onto the floor behind the pilot's seat.

"Sorry sir,' she gasped. 'What has happened?"

"Bird strike," the pilot told her. "We've lost two engines and it sounds as though the other two are being starved of fuel. The starboard flaps aren't responding at all. I can't get her nose up." He reached for the intercom switch. "Seat belts! She's going down."

'No one in the cabin would have heard that message,' Aunt Sandra said. 'The intercom system had also been knocked out. The captain didn't know this at the time, of course, but he told the air hostess to go and fetch the first officer. She couldn't. The flight-deck door was now jammed shut.'

"*Mayday, Mayday. This is-*"

That was as far as the pilot got with his emergency call. In fact that was the last anyone heard from that Bristol Britannia airliner.'

Thomas gasped. 'So... what happened? What comes next.'

Aunt Sandra shook her head and frowned. 'What do *you* think comes next, Thomas.'

The boy stared at her, his face a mixture of sorrow and confusion.

'I don't know... it sounds like the end. What does come after that, auntie?'

Sandra Quinn sighed and pulled her wheelchair closer to the table. After taking a sip of water she said, 'I'll be learning the answer to that one soon enough, Tommy.'

Thomas Carrol stared expectantly at his aunt, waiting for an explanation that did not come. Eventually he climbed down from the bed and went to join her at the table. He reached out for her hand, careful not to put pressure on her knobbly fingers.

'But auntie... it's your story. You can change the end to be whatever you like.'

Sandra Quinn smiled. 'That's what I do when I make up stories, Thomas. With made up stories, either the writer chooses the ending or leaves it for the reader to decide. But this one is a true story, so it should only say what the writer knows for sure is true. In true stories there's no room for rumour or speculation. That means there must be no assumptions and no guesswork either.'

The boy closed his eyes and thought for a few moments. 'Then I suppose whatever's definitely true must be the right ending,' he said. 'Like the news on television and in the newspapers?'

Aunt Sandra chuckled. 'Ah yes... the newspapers. Bring me my cuttings book, please, Thomas.'

The boy leapt up and rushed to the dressing table. From a shallow drawer below the mirror, he took out a padded photograph album. Placing it carefully on the small round table, he watched intently as his aunt opened the book and leafed through the first few pages. Thomas had seen some of the cuttings before, when one of auntie's stories had been about tennis. It was that story and those newspaper cuttings that had inspired the children to ask for their own racquets last Christmas, since when they had played for at least an hour a day every weekend whenever the weather permitted.

Sandra Quinn had told the twins that she had once been a very good tennis player, although she had corrected Geraldine when the girl had described her as famous. 'Not famous, dear,' she had said. 'Well known, perhaps, but only briefly.' But the proof was there, in the cuttings book. Their aunt had once got through to the second round at Wimbledon, and her picture had even been on the back pages of some of the newspapers.

'Things were different then,' she had told them. 'The players were all amateurs, and unless they had wealthy parents they had to work, not just for a living but also to cover the cost of their tennis kit, travel and accommodation.'

After leaving school Aunt Sandra had made her living as a newspaper photographer, using the by-line Sandy Quinton. 'There was terrible discrimination in those days,' she had told the twins. 'My pictures probably wouldn't even have been considered if the editors had realised who I was. Not only was I an Irish immigrant but I was also a woman. Press photographer simply wasn't a woman's career, so they just assumed that Sandy Quinton was a man. Things are better now, but they're still not right.'

Thomas loved hearing his aunt talk about her long and exciting life. 'I do hope that Ger and I can have adventures like yours,' he had told her.

The old lady had thought about that for a few moments before replying. 'Adventures... yes. I suppose that's what they were. Extraordinary parts of an otherwise ordinary life. But once an adventure is over that's the end of it. If you tried to have the same adventure again, it wouldn't be an adventure. It would have become... well, ordinary. That's why you two can't have adventures like mine.'

Thomas had nodded slowly and then smiled. 'But we can have exciting adventures of our own, can't we?'

'Yes, you certainly can my dears.'

'So what is there in between the adventures?' Geraldine had asked. 'And afterwards. There must be something.'

Sandra Quinn was harking back to that conversation now. 'Remember what I told you and your sister about adventures? When they're over they are gone forever. Afterwards what you are left with are memories. But occasionally there are also other people's published accounts of your adventures. Here...'

Skimming over the next few pages of cuttings, Sandra turned to a black-and-white photograph of two women in smart uniforms. That's me with one of my friends. We were always referred to as air hostesses in those days. Nowadays it's no longer only a woman's job. Men *and* women work as what are called cabin crew.'

'Who is she?' Thomas asked. 'The other lady.'

'That's Yvonne. We worked together a couple of times while we were air hostesses. Later on we both became pilots. I wasn't the first British woman to get an airline pilot's licence. That was Yvonne. Her full name was Yvonne Pope Sintes. We both flew passenger planes. Now that really *was* an adventure.'

'Wow!' Thomas said, peering out at the summer sky.

'But about two years before Yvonne qualified as a pilot,' Aunt Sandra whispered in a conspiratorial *don't-tell-another-soul* kind of voice, 'I actually flew an airliner over the Swiss Alps for at least ten minutes, maybe more. So perhaps I could claim to be the first British woman to fly an airliner... although there were no passengers on board, so maybe it doesn't really count.'

'It counts with *me*,' Thomas said. 'But... someone else must have known. It would have been in the newspapers, surely.'

'The newspaper account is right here, in my book of clippings. Would you like to read it to me, Thomas?'

Sandra Quinn turned to a page with three separate newspaper headlines, all about the same event. *Courageous Pilot Dies Saving Colleagues*, one headline read; *Airplane Accident Averted*, said another; and *Crew Saved but Brave Pilot Dies*. There was only one report, because the same account had appeared in all the newspapers, so Sandra had clipped out just the one copy.

The boy nodded, moved his chair closer to his aunt, and began, *"Airline pilot Captain Geoffrey Isaacson (39) was piloting a BOAC airliner from Rome to London, where it was due to be decommissioned. While over the Swiss Alps, a large bird flew into one of the propellers. The resulting debris destroyed a second engine and jammed one of the wing flaps. The co-pilot, First Officer Timothy Jacobs (35), incurred a severe head wound in the collision and was rendered unconscious. The only other people onboard were two BOAC air hostesses.*

"Skilfully keeping the crippled aircraft in a tight spiral turn, the captain managed to land the plane on a small plateau, pulling up just

yards before a sheer rock cliff face. When rescuers reached the damaged airliner they found only three survivors. Captain Isaacson had suffered a massive heart attack and was pronounced dead at the scene.

"In a tribute to Captain Isaacson, who was unmarried and lived alone in a south London flat, the chairman of BOAC described him as a gifted, courageous and generous man who would be greatly missed."

Thomas Carrol sat in silence for a few moments. 'He was a hero, wasn't he, auntie? He saved three other people's lives. Did you ever meet him?'

'Yes, I did, dear. Would you like to hear my account of our meeting?'

'Ooh, yes please auntie. Will you write it as a story?'

Aunt Sandra chuckled. 'I wrote the story several years ago. Here it is,' and she pulled out three loose pages from the back of the book. They were neatly handwritten in blue ink on cream paper.

'At the age of 32, I applied for a job as a BOAC air hostess. I was tall, slim and spoke clearly with only a slight Irish accent.'

The old lady looked up from her written script. 'I was also good looking, and in those days, my dear, I'm sorry to say looks mattered more than anything else in those kinds of jobs.'

Returning to her notes, Sandra Quinn continued, 'Anyway, I got the job, which is where I met Yvonne Pope Sintes. Yvonne was later to become famous as Britain's first woman airline pilot. But my best friend while I worked for BOAC was Claire Fowler. Claire was a few years older than me, and she helped me a lot when I was getting started. We teamed up regularly on flights across Europe, and it was through Claire that I came to meet Captain Geoffrey Isaacson, the pilot in the newspaper story.

'The three of us had been in Rome for a long weekend, me, Clare and her boyfriend Geoffrey, and we weren't due to fly back to London until the following Tuesday morning. Anyway, that Sunday morning Geoff had proposed to Claire at the Fountain of Trevi. It was all very romantic, and they were so happy. But then our travel plans had to be changed. That Sunday evening, the company phoned our hotel asking us to crew an old airliner that was being brought back to England for decommissioning. That means broken up for scrap, dear.'

'Decommissioning... okay,' Thomas said. He enjoyed learning new words, especially big ones.

'Well, you already know quite a lot of the story. Claire and I were the two air hostesses involved in that plane crash. So... we were over the Swiss mountains when an eagle - or maybe it was a vulture - flew into one of the propellers. The engine exploded and the debris damaged another of the engines and jammed the port aileron. Oh... in case that's a word you don't know, Thomas, an aileron is the metal flap on the edge of a wing that moves up or down to make the aircraft bank when it is turning. Tim was badly injured and-'

'It didn't say *any* of this in the newspaper,' Thomas interrupted, frowning at the press cutting accusingly. 'I thought the news was supposed to be the truth. You and Claire aren't named either. Why not?'

Aunt Sandra shrugged. 'It's just an account, Thomas. No account is ever the full story. News stories include only what the writer decides is important, and in this incident the names of the air hostesses were considered unnecessary details. Anyway, as I was saying, Tim Jacobs, the first officer, had been knocked unconscious and was bleeding badly, so while Claire bandaged him up I went to check that captain Isaacson was okay. I found him wrenching at the controls and calling for Tim to come and help him. Then, just as I had asked what had gone wrong, the plane went into a steep dive, the cockpit door slammed shut, and I ended up on my backside, battered and bruised, squashed behind the pilot's seat.'

The old lady was no longer reading from her notes. She too was gazing out at the summer sky as though the full story was written there in invisible ink.

'As I hauled myself up, the captain let out a terrible groan and clutched at his chest saying, "Tell Claire. I'm sorry. I love-" He never finished that sentence. His hands dropped down to the controls, and his chin flopped onto his chest.'

Thomas Carrol had been holding his breath. He gasped. 'Then what?'

'I didn't know what to do,' his aunt continued, 'but I had to try *something*. I could see that we were heading for the steep side of a mountain. I reached forward, put my hands on top of the captain's and tried to move the control column to the right. The plane turned more sharply towards the mountain, so I pushed the controls the other way, and the plane veered away from the rock face. That was very nearly the end for all of us, Thomas.'

'Weren't you scared, auntie?'

Sandra Quinn nodded. 'Oh yes, dear. I have never been more scared. But over the next ten minutes or so, by trial and error I learned how to keep the plane going around in circles between the two sides of the deep valley. We were losing height rapidly, and the ground seemed to be rushing up to meet us. Then I thought I heard someone whisper "pull", but I'm not sure. I might just have imagined it. Anyway, I tried it. Pulling back on the control column didn't take us out of the dive completely, but it slowed our descent, so much so that when the plane hit the ground it didn't break up or burst into flames. Although the undercarriage had collapsed, the fuselage remained intact. We skidded along leaving a half-mile scar on the flowery valley floor, until the plane came to rest with its nose almost within touching distance of a steep rocky slope.'

Thomas Carrol let out a long sigh of relief. Aunt Sandra glanced at him and smiled before she continued, now back to reading from her notes. 'As I let go of the captain's hands, I was convinced that I heard someone whisper, "Well done," but again... had I just imagined it?

'When rescuers arrived it took them a while to find tools that would open the door to the flight deck. By that time, Claire, who had been caring for the first officer, had been taken with him to the hospital, so she had no idea what had happened to Geoffrey and me. It turned out that I had three broken ribs and was suffering from mild concussion, so I was also taken to hospital. When I saw Claire the next day she had heard the news about Geoff and she was in shock. Her fiancée had been pronounced dead at the crash site.'

'So who wrote this newspaper account? You, or Claire?' Thomas asked.

'Neither of us, dear,' Aunt Sandra replied. 'It came from the BOAC publicity office, and because women didn't fly airliners in those days they came to what they thought was the only logical conclusion, that the pilot had landed the aircraft just before he died.'

The boy was frowning and shaking his head. 'But... why didn't you write to the newspapers and tell them what *really* happened, auntie? It was you who saved the plane and the crew.'

'Ah, but can we be sure about that?' Aunt Sandra asked. 'Or had Captain Isaacson whispered guidance to me with his dying breath? We will never know for certain. But also... think how terrible it must have been for Claire, her husband-to-be dying just two days after they had become engaged.'

'Oh yes, auntie.' Thomas said. 'She must have been very sad.'

Aunt Sandra nodded. 'Do you think it would have been a comfort to Claire to hear that her fiancée had died while saving her life, and mine and Tim's too?'

The young boy sat in deep thought for quite a while. Then he looked out at the sky again. 'Yes, I do, and it's right that Claire should be proud of him. He *was* a hero.'

Then, pushing back a tear, the young boy gave his aunt a gentle hug. 'And so are you, auntie,' he said. 'And I shall always be proud of you.'

The old lady chuckled. 'Enough, now... be off with you Tommy Carrol and give your sister a proper game of tennis before she wears the last of the net paint off my wall.'

Once the boy had left, Sandra Quinn reached for the three handwritten cream pages. She tore them into tiny pieces and dropped them into the waste-paper bin.

-oo0oo-

12 A Window on Conscience

'Can I help you, sir?' the shop assistant said with a smile, as he slipped his phone into the back pocket of his purple jeans and came out from behind the sales counter. 'Looking for something in particular, or just browsing?'

It was only ten past nine and Darren was saving what little work there was so he could look busy if the manager arrived early, although at this time of year she rarely appeared before lunchtime. Two months ago they had been rushed off their feet from nine 'til five. But now, in October, seeing even a solitary customer before 10 a.m. was a rare occurrence.

'Warm dressing gowns,' the tall man said, without meeting the youth's gaze. '*A* warm dressing gown, that is,' he added.

The tall man was wearing a crumpled grey shirt, grey trousers and scuffed black boots with white laces. Unlikely to be a big spender, Darren thought.

'For someone special?' he prompted, trying again with his smile.

'Yes. It's for me.'

He had hoped that his old dressing gown would see him out, but a freak gust of wind had blown it off the clothes line and into the dense copse of sea buckthorn that separated the garden of Garth House from the eroding cliffs that would one day claim the whole plot. Not that he cared a jot. Like me it's a crumbling old ruin, he thought. I've no one close to bequeath it to, or to persecute in any other way.

What insane impulse had led him to wash his dressing gown after all those years? Never again! When he had snatched the old multi-coloured garment from its resting place, the thorn bushes looked as though they were decorated with Tibetan prayer flags. All he had been left with was a useless piece of tattered lace. This time he would buy something more suited to his mood. Ah, yes, this would do. A really drab shade of grey.

'Like to try it on, sir. We have a fitting room with a mirror over-'

'No need for that.'

He pulled on the dressing gown over his shirt. 'Seems to fit,' he said. Checking the label, he added, 'Medium? What's that supposed to mean. A dubious claim for psychic powers?'

Darren had little time to puzzle over this obscure remark. Someone else had entered the shop. An old man in a long dark overcoat. He turned to the newcomer. 'Can I help you?'

The newcomer smiled. 'Just browsing, thank you.'

Darren turned back to his first customer of the day. 'You look really smart in it, sir. Very... distinguished.'

'Irrelevant,' he snapped. 'No one else is likely to see it. Not until I'm *ex*tinguished.'

'Oh dear,' the boy replied. 'I hope I haven't said something to upset you, sir.'

The customer sighed ostentatiously. 'You couldn't if you tried. You just haven't got it in you.'

The man in the overcoat stopped thumbing through clothes on the sale rail. He nodded several times, turned and smiled sympathetically at the sales assistant but made no comment.

'Shall I wrap it up it for you, sir?' Darren asked quickly, unable to rekindle his smile.

The customer nodded but made no reply.

Darren felt uneasy in the frosty silence. Folding the dressing gown neatly, he tried again. 'Are you a local or just visiting, sir?'

'So, you prefer locals to visitors. Why is that?'

'I... I don't understand...'

'Well, if *you* don't understand what you have said, maybe I can make it crystal clear to you. You *could* have said, "*Are you visiting or just a local?*" That would imply that you favoured visitors. But you didn't, so I'll ask you again. Why do you prefer locals to visitors? Is it a matter of who spends the most money? Self interest! Greed! Right?'

The young man frowned and looked at his shoes. 'I didn't mean *anything* by it, sir. I'm sorry if I-'

Stuffing the dressing gown into an old paper bag, the shop assistant thrust it towards the customer and said. 'That will be thirty pounds, please.'

'Extortionate!' the tall man retorted. He handed over the money and stormed out of the shop, pushing past the man in the long dark overcoat.

'Another person's day blighted by your unique ability to spread misery wherever you go.'

The departing customer turned to retaliate, but his critic had vanished. Where to? Back into the shop to try and console the stupid idiot? He shrugged and walked away.

~~~

Sitting in his study at Garth House, the tall man stared through the French windows to the swaying sea buckthorn bushes at the end of his garden. Fragments of his old dressing gown were still fluttering in the breeze.

He glanced across at the desk, where he had dumped the bag containing his latest purchase. If it had been my shop, he thought, I would never have employed such a spotty-faced illiterate dimwit. What had he written on his name badge? Not Darren, but *Darrin*. Pathetic! He can't even be trusted to write his own name correctly.

The tall man turned back to the window. Someone was standing among the bushes, half obscured by the drizzle. Then he recognised the intruder – well, not quite an intruder, but borderline. It was that man in the long dark overcoat. He himself had a very similar coat hanging behind his kitchen door. Stupid twit's going to need that if the weather forecast proves accurate. Drizzle at least until midnight, and probably more to come tomorrow. Everything and everyone outside would soon be dripping wet. He thought again about the pathetic sales assistant in the clothes shop. He was the other kind of wet drip, head full of nothing but idle chatter. He had only got what he deserved.

The tall man glanced at the clock on the wall. Nearly time for tea. It would be getting dark soon, and it was definitely not an evening to be out on the cliff tops. He looked out across the lawn. For the second time that day the man in the long dark overcoat had moved off. Good riddance! Some folk seem to have nothing better to do than poke their noses in where they are not wanted.

A shiver ran down the tall man's spine. He grabbed the bag and, tearing it open, shook out the grey dressing gown and put it on. That's better, he thought as he threw down the useless bag that the useless sales assistant had packed so clumsily. Stupid idiot!

He sat down again and checked the garden. The man in the long dark overcoat had reappeared. He was now standing on the far side of the lawn. This *is* an intrusion, he thought, and not one I'm going to take lying down. Unlike that pathetic wimp in the clothes shop, who lacks the backbone to stand up for himself. Why would anyone choose to side with such an empty-headed youth with his mindless meanderings?

Two minutes later, the tall man had returned from his scullery with a double-barrel shotgun and a handful of cartridges. This calls for a show of strength on my part, he muttered to himself. If he comes much closer I'll make sure he gets the message, loud and clear.

Seated on the edge of the desk, he pointed the shotgun towards the intruder. The man in the overcoat shrugged again. He walked towards the house, stopping in the middle of the lawn, where he nodded and smiled, as he had done in the shop. The tall man slipped the catch on the French windows and opened them slightly. 'Clear off. D'you hear me? Leave me alone, or else...'

'Or else?' the intruder replied. 'Ah, yes. You do still have options, although you are closing them down rapidly. But think of this... for many people there isn't an *or else*. They have no alternatives.'

'I don't know what-.' The thin man stopped himself. I'm not so stupid as to fall into that little trap, he told himself.

'You have the ability to understand, if you choose to,' the intruder said. 'Do you *really* think the boy in the shop could have opted to have a better brain? Should he have chosen parents who, like yours, could afford to buy him the best education possible?'

'I don't have to listen to all this-'

'You heard. And what's said and heard can't be undone. Your first line of defence, choosing not to listen, has already been overrun. Your last ditch strategy, not to think about it, is also failing you. That poor young lad will have spent most of yesterday thinking and feeling bad about his limitations. Limitations over which he has no control. How are you coping with yours, which are entirely self-inflicted? Think about that.'

The two men stared at each other until the owner of the house decided to act. He went back into the kitchen and returned with a length of strong string. Then, having wedged the gun between the desk and a heavy armchair so that the barrels pointed at the centre of the French windows, he tied one end of the string around both triggers. Hooking the string over a drawer handle, he secured the other end to a catch on the French windows.

'It won't be my fault', the tall man shouted into a now empty garden. 'If you chose to enter, you will get both barrels. And deservedly so. Just like that stupid oaf in the shop deserved what *he* got.'

He paused. The man in the long dark overcoat was back. He was now standing just a couple of paces from the French windows.

'I had a perfect right to pick him up on his abuse of the English language,' the tall man shouted. 'Just as I have a perfect right to protect myself and my own property if I chose to do so. It's my choice... Oh, damn it! I fell right into your damned trap, didn't I?'

The man in the long dark overcoat nodded. 'You certainly did.'

'Why can't you leave me alone? For the life of me I can't think what I've done to hurt *you*.'

The face outside the window smiled. 'For the life of you... yes. But in the end you certainly will have to think. When you intentionally hurt that poor boy you damaged yourself. Your victim will get over it. I'm here to make sure that you won't.'

A shadow of doubt flickered across the tall man's face and got stuck there. 'I don't understand...' he began.

'Well, if you don't understand what you have said, I had better come in and explain it to you in a way that you *will* understand without a shadow of doubt. It will be crystal clear, I promise.'

~~~

'I've checked the lawns all around the house sir. No footprints, so although the French windows were open I reckon we can rule out foul play, attempted burglary and the like.'

'Agreed, sergeant. Two shredded dressing gowns, and one wasted life. It's an open and shut case. Or should that be casement.' The Inspector chuckled at his own off-the-cuff witticism. 'Damned elaborate set up, but a crystal clear case of suicide, without a shadow of doubt.'

-oo0oo-

13 Fear

Steve Delmonte's earliest memories were of fear of the dark. What child has not imagined twilight terrors, monsters more menacing for their invisibility? But now, constrained, confined, bitterly cold, and in total blackness with no idea where he was or how he came to be there, the fear this middle-aged man felt was absolute, solid, impenetrable. Tears streamed from his unseeing eyes as his hands clawed at the unyielding barrier directly above his face. The screech of fingernails on rough timber was muted by blood from the raw flesh of his skinless fingertips. His legs were useless in a space so narrow that he couldn't bend his knees to push or kick at anything. If only that deafening noise would stop, someone might just hear his screams.

Then he was moving, being shaken from side to side. And that deafening noise, like the booming bass of muffled music. What was it? But now he could smell something. Smoke? Yes. And something else, too. He was suffocating, and he was no longer cold. He was hot, much too hot. One more try: 'Help me, Lil. Get me out.'

'Wake up, Steve. *Steve!*' Lily Delmonte was out of bed and shaking her husband as hard as she could. His eyes opened.

'You've had one of your nightmares, my love. You're sweating like a pig. Sit up. I'll go and get you a cold drink.'

'No, Lil. Don't leave me. Please, not yet.'

Lily Delmonte sat on the edge of the coffee table and reached for her husband's hand, as she had done countless times since he started having these nightmares nearly two years ago, just after Bianca was born. 'You're okay now, Steve. But there's no point in either of us trying to go back to sleep. It's nearly time to get up anyway. Jim and Carla will be here in six hours' time, and I want to do something special for our first lunch together. It's been nearly a year since they came over and we all had Christmas in Salisbury. Bianca was just starting to walk then, remember? She's talking now, Carla says. English *and* Italian.'

Steve Delmonte hadn't been listening. 'It was awful, Lil. Worse than ever, and I now know why. I'm in a coffin. I'm being taken to the crematorium, but I'm still alive.'

Lily stared at him, suddenly afraid that her husband's nightmares were driving him insane. Before she could formulate a meaningful response he continued, 'That noise. It could be the music. In my will, remember? House of the Rising Sun. It drowns out my screaming. Nobody can hear me. And then I can smell my hair and my skin starting to burn. And then-'

'And then I woke you up, Steve. So now you know it was just a dream. A very bad dream. But that's all it was.'

They sat in silence for a few moments and then he started again. 'I was… no. Listen, Lil, please. I was thinking. When we get back home I'm going to change my will. No music. Just silence. Okay? And I want *two* doctors to certify independently that I'm really dead.'

'*Steve*!' Lil Delmonte shouted. 'Don't you ever stop to think what your fixation on dying is doing to me and the family. You're forty-nine not ninety-four, for God's sake. Jim and Carla will be bringing your two-year-old granddaughter here in a few hours' time. Are you going to scare the living daylights out them, too, with this kind of stuff for the rest of our holiday?'

The winter sun was rising as Steve Delmonte sat up in bed. He stared across the top of the long coffee table and out of the big picture window. Beyond the frosted rooftops of a mishmash of modest single-story homes lining the narrow road to Jim and Carla's two-story house and then on up to the old church in the village square, mist was rising from the broad plateau of Castellucio. Now only vaguely delineated into strips of various shades of brown, three months from now the plateau would be an artist's pallet of reds, yellows, and blues as poppies, daisies and cornflowers mingle with the lentil crops for which the region is renowned. He shook his head. 'Sorry Lil,' he said. 'No. I'm okay now. But it all seemed so real. It's more frightening every time. It's getting so bad I'm scared to go to sleep in case-'

'Yes I know, Steve. I just wish there was something I could do to help, but there isn't. Dr Mason says most people who have your kind of nightmares eventually find something that breaks the chain. Maybe this holiday will do the trick, especially once the family get back from Frankfurt, after the Book Fair.' Lil Delmonte gave her husband' arm another squeeze. 'You lie back and relax while I go and make us some coffee.'

Glancing again at the road leading up from the valley floor, Steve Delmonte was dazzled momentarily by sunlight reflecting from the polished oak coffee table. This was no ordinary table, his Grandfather Guiseppe had told him. With its massive legs and its solid oak top and end panels, it doubled as an air raid shelter - or it would have done had the Second World War spilled into that remote part of Italy. Jim always said he hated having a coffee table as the centrepiece of his bedroom; but, assembled decades ago where it now stood between the old bed and the new picture window, the oak monstrosity was too big and much too heavy to move.

Guiseppe Delmonte had been a master craftsman. He had built the house and most of the furniture, but the solid rock and sparse covering of soil of the hill slope precluded a cellar, and there was no space for a separate shelter. So, ever resourceful, Guiseppe had made a matching pair of tables-cum-shelters, one for himself in the main bedroom and another, on the ground floor, for his wife Francesca.

When Francesca had died, in 1979, Steve's father Antonio had inherited the house. By that time Antonio had a family and a career in Salisbury, where Steve had been born, so The House On The Hill, as they called it, had been rented out as a holiday home, popular with botanists and birdwatchers. Then Steve and Lily's son Jim had met and married Carla. As an environmental writer Jim could work from anywhere, and so he and Carla had moved into The House On The Hill, just a fifteen-minute drive from Carla's coffee shop on the outskirts of San Pellegrino.

The sound of footsteps on the stairs told Steve that his wife was on the way up with the coffee. He groaned as the bedside light flickered and went out. Yet another power cut. Still, the sun was coming up, and so was the coffee.

He watched as Lily placed the steaming cup onto a coaster. 'This'll get you going, Steve,' she said with a grin. She turned and strolled across to the picture window. 'I never get tired of this view. Even in winter, it's just amazing.'

Steve glanced down the road. Rooftops on the edge of the village were shimmering in the sunlight. Tiles appeared to be falling from the roofs and shattering on the road. A trick of the light? More tiles fell into a crevasse that had opened up in the road. People were running from the houses, their shouts and screams now audible through the gaping hole where the picture window had been.

'Lily! Get under the-'

Steve Delmonte stared in disbelief as his wife turned to him and descended as though in an elevator. The front wall of the bedroom, with its broken window, had collapsed outwards. He heard more glass shattering and people screaming. Crawling to the ragged edge of his bedroom floor, he stared down at the heap of rubble that had once been the front of The House On The Hill. Lily was staggering down the road towards a group of stunned neighbours. He breathed a sigh of relief. She was okay. The house shook again and pieces of plaster rained down from the ceiling, one narrowly missing his head. He dropped to the floor and slid beneath the coffee table just as huge chunks of plaster and roof tiles began cascading onto the bed, the floor, the coffee table. Then the rafters collapsed, and their weight pushed the table legs through the bedroom floor, the end panels setting the gap between the table top and the floor just deep enough to avoid crushing his head. The weight on his chest made it almost impossible to breathe. He could still see out to where the other homes used to be. Not one was left standing. Another tremor… another pile of debris crashed down onto the oak plank that separated him from oblivion. The floor tilted and he could now see through a dusty haze to the broad plateau in the distance. The road *had* collapsed. No rescue vehicles would be coming in that way, and there was no other overland route into the village.

All day he had lain there, gasping for breath, unable to cry out. Watching. Waiting. Hearing the shouts of villagers desperately digging through the rubble in search of survivors. The sun was now setting. With electricity cut off, darkness would soon descend bringing with it the biting frost of a midwinter night in Umbria. He could smell smoke. People were lighting fires, but not just to keep warm. They needed to see what they were doing. All along the street, fires were now blazing, people dragging timber from the wreckage to keep them going. He felt a hint of warmth from a fire directly across the road, and then he heard a rumbling noise. A tractor. He watched as it clambered over a mound of rubble that had once been his neighbour's house. A huge fork lift on the front of the machine hoisted an old roof beam from the debris, turned, and dumped it onto the fire. Sparks flew into the night sky, and the fire gained strength. Three more beams were added to the fire, and then the driver turned the machine towards what was left of the two-story house. Steve Delmonte couldn't see what was happening, but when the tractor backed away beams and rafters were hanging from the forks, and the driver lowered them onto the fire. *That should give light for a couple of hours,* Steve told himself. *Plenty of time for rescuers to find me.*

The steel forks turned again towards the remains of The House On The Hill. Then Steve Delmonte was being hoisted into the air, still with the oak table on top of him and a huge section of bedroom floor beneath him. The tractor backed away from the house. *Just lower me gently,* he thought, *and I'll be back safe and sound with my Lil.*

But he was still being lifted, not lowered. Smoke swirled around him and his eyes began streaming. His hands clawed at the impenetrable barrier directly above his face, and the scrape of his fingernails on solid timber told him that the wetness he felt was blood from the raw flesh of his skinless fingertips. His legs were useless in a space so narrow that he couldn't bend his knees to push or kick at anything. If only that deafening tractor noise would stop, surely someone would hear his screams. And that smell: he knew what it was now. Singeing hair and scorching skin. He was being burned alive.

The shaking became more violent. 'Steve! Steve, for God's sake wake up.'

'What? Oh, Lil. You're safe. We're both safe.' He was shivering and sweat was pouring from his brow.

'You nodded off again in the few minutes it took me to go and make coffee, Steve. Maybe we *do* need to get you to a doctor.'

'It's okay, Lil. Just a nightmare. I'll be fine now. But we've to go and meet Jim and Carla.'

'And Bianca,' his wife replied. 'That's what I wanted us to do, but you were adamant we should stay here and wait for them. Anyway, we've still got more than enough time to get to the airport.'

'Let's book us all into a really nice hotel, Lil. A couple of days in Rome. As a surprise.'

Lily Delmonte gave her husband a puzzled stare. 'So what earth-shattering revelation has brought on this sudden change of heart?'

'Nothing. Nothing yet.'

~~~

Flight LH242 from Frankfurt had landed, but with no gate available the passengers were waiting for an airport bus to take them to the terminal building. Jim Delmonte switched on his phone and called his folks. No answer. He checked his emails. Nothing. He then tuned into the BBC World Service and was astonished to hear his mother's voice.

'"*It was all so unexpected, except that… I'm sorry, I can't explain…*"

That was our BBC Rome correspondent talking with Steve and Lily Delmonte, who had left the village shortly before the devastating earthquake struck.'

-ooOoo-

14 Villain, Victim, Victor

Sharon Willis got out of bed and lurched, leaning against the wall. It wasn't frightening any more. She knew what to do. Just take deep breaths and wait until the head clears and the room stops swimming. Sitting on the edge of the bed she pushed a Stemetil tablet from the blister pack and gulped it down. Her hands were shaking. Give it five minutes, she told herself. Then she would be able to shower, check emails and get ready for work.

The first time it had happened was scary. Dr Kowalski did blood tests, checked for something called labyrinthitis and then arranged an MRI scan. All clear. No sign of a brain tumour, which was a huge relief. He had eventually concluded that it must be a side effect of her getting two variants of covid within four months. Sharon knew three other people who were suffering from long covid, and they were all affected more seriously than she was. She considered herself lucky. The attacks had become less frequent, several weeks apart now. The pills pretty much fixed the dizziness and the brain fog, although not the tiredness which at times bordered on exhaustion. She had to battle through that and not let it affect her work, at least not so that anyone else could tell. And so far she had succeeded. Except once, when it had almost certainly cost her a promotion. But if she'd told them why she'd had a dizzy turn it would probably have been the end of her career – in CID at least.

Two years ago she'd had a wobble when she got out of bed, and with her promotion board scheduled for 11.30 she had taken a double dose of Stemetils. Dr Kowalski had told her that would be quite okay if she got a really bad attack. All had been fine until she entered the interview room. The super – not Ken Wilberforce but his predecessor Imran Bukhari, who had retired a few weeks later – waved her to a chair. She turned, had one of her wobbles, and fell heavily against the boardroom table.

'Are you feeling okay, constable?'

She should have said no. She knew that now. But she had waited three years for the chance of promotion, and she had sailed through all the exams with distinction. The board interview should have been a mere formality.

'No. I mean yes, I'm fine sir, sorry.' She had looked around the room, and for a moment she couldn't think why she was in there, but she sat down and tried to breathe deeply.

'Sharon…' the superintendent was saying. 'I asked you a question.'

'Sorry sir. I… I missed that.'

'I asked how long you had been in CID and what you enjoy most about the work.'

'Yes sir.' Sharon could hear that she was slurring her words. She shook her head. 'Yes, I really do enjoy the work. It's what I've always wanted to do.'

Another board member chipped in, 'Constable Willis. I want you to answer this question frankly. Have you got a drink problem?'

The superintendent glowered at his colleague but said nothing.

'No sir. I haven't. I never did.'

DI Karen Hertz held up her hand, and the super nodded.

'What would you say is the greatest talent you bring to CID, and how do you make use of it.'

Sharon stared back at the DI. She tried to formulate an answer but her head was spinning. 'I'm sorry,' she said. 'I can't think of anything in particular. I'm very good at my job, though.'

'Maybe you should stick with it, then,' DI Hertz said flatly, and she closed her notebook with an air of finality that even Sharon's fuddled mind could not fail to comprehend.

And that had been it. Two more years as a DC, fortunately with one of the best DIs in the force as her line manager. DI Mike Horton was due to retire in a year's time, and Sharon was desperately hoping to get through a sergeant's board before then.

Was it work pressure that brought on these attacks? Probably not. She'd come through some pretty challenging cases with Mike in the last year or so, and at no time had her problem manifested itself at work. It's not stress related, just random, she had concluded.

Sharon looked at her bedside clock. Twenty past seven. Better get going, she thought, hauling herself upright. Steady? Yes, okay now. Time for a shower.

As Sharon was drying her hair, her work phone rang. 'DC Wallis.'

'Sharon? It's Mike. We've had a call from a distressed couple, John and Margaret Dawson. They've had a break in at their flat in Fallon Towers. Know it?'

'Fallon Towers… yes of course. Posh flats. Ten minutes drive from here.' She checked her watch. Twenty-five to eight. 'I can be there by ten to eight, maybe a few minutes before. I'll meet you there. Okay?'

'Actually, I've got to get mum sorted first, so you'll be there well ahead of me. Just go in, calm them down and take down the essentials. Stay with them until I can join you. Thieves rarely hang around longer than necessary, but let's not take any risks. We'll check the other flats together. I'll let the duty officer know what we're going to do.'

Sharon drove past Fallon Towers twice a day on her way to and from the station, but she had never been inside. Despite the plural, there was only the one tower. Built about ten years ago, the three-story block of luxury flats stood in incongruous isolation on the banks of the River Severn just outside the city boundary.

~~~

'I just need to make a few notes. The message I got said you've had a break in. Flat one, is that right?'

John Dawson, a middle-aged man with a striking shock of curly white hair, merely nodded. His wife, quite a few years younger Sharon thought, turned her wheelchair towards the detective, gave her a half smile and said, 'Just call me Marge. Everyone else does.'

Sharon checked her watch and recorded the time in her notebook. Ten to eight. 'Okay, Marge. Thanks.'

The woman nodded her head and continued. 'We've only been here three days. We're renting the flat for a week while our daughter has treatment in the Royal. I made the booking online, and the keys were posted to us. The owner's spending the winter in Greece.'

'Corfu,' John Dawson said.

'That *is* part of Greece,' his wife snapped irritably. Her husband sat back in his chair and stared at the ceiling.

'Do you know who lives in the other eight flats, Marge?'

'No, not really. Well, I say that. I did meet the young man from number four. That's the flat directly above ours. I was in the hallway, and John was fetching our suitcase from the car. Faisal Malik, I think he said he was. Or something like that. I was a bit preoccupied, and I'm sure he realised it. He only said hello. Didn't stop. I assumed he was setting off for work.'

'Have *you* met any of the others, John?' Sharon asked.

The husband paused, frowned and then shook his head. 'I know the bloke Marge is on about. Not to speak to, but I saw him leaving here about eleven o'clock yesterday morning. Maybe he works late shifts. The only others I've seen are what looks like a mother with a teenage daughter. I think they're in either five or six, on the second floor.'

That still leaves six other flats not accounted for, Sharon mused.

The woman was talking again. 'We've never been much into socialising, John and me.'

'No matter,' Sharon said. 'As soon as Inspector Horton gets here we'll check with your neighbours, just to make sure they're all okay.'

'How long will he be?' the woman asked.

Sharon was peering at her phone. 'Well... he's just texted me to say he's setting off now. So probably half an hour, maybe a bit more. He's coming from the other side of the city. But don't worry. I'll be staying with you until he gets here. Before we leave you we'll need to be absolutely sure the intruder is no longer in the building.'

'Half an hour,' Mrs Dawson repeated and glanced at her husband. He nodded but made no comment.

'So... What alerted you? The alarm?'

'No,' the woman replied. 'The alarm wasn't on. Wish I *had* set it. But I mean, I didn't see any need unless we were going to be out. Mostly I'm indoors because of... well, this.' She pointed at her wheelchair. 'Even at home, I make a list and then John does the shopping.'

Sharon frowned but made no reply. Probably best not to ask, she thought. The woman shrugged and continued, 'So, when I came into the sitting room at... let's see now, that must have have been getting on for half past seven. Yes, that's right. I knew immediately someone had been in. The drawer and doors of the sideboard were open. I would never leave them like that. So I called John and we checked everything.'

The detective was writing in her notebook. 'What's missing?'

'The door to the flat was wide open,' Marge said. 'They weren't ours, but two candlesticks have gone. Silvery, but most likely only chrome plated. They were on the mantelpiece. And my pearl earrings are missing too. I'd put them in the sideboard drawer.'

'Not in a safe?'

'They're not genuine. Not worth anything.' Margaret Dawson gave the detective a wry smile, and Sharon noticed that the husband was now staring down at his feet. Was his wife implying he was a miserly old cheapskate? Sharon had to let that thought take flight, because Marge was in full flow again. 'I brought my mother's diamond brooch with us, two carats. There's a safe in the bedroom, so I locked it in there. We checked. It's still there. So that's when we phoned 999 and shut ourselves in 'til we saw you arrive.'

'As far as I can see there's no sign of forced entry,' Sharon said. 'The door's not damaged and the windows are all locked and no panes broken.' The DC paused and then added, 'So, either the intruder knew how to pick your lock or he had a key. Or she. So, other than you, who else has a key to the flat?'

'Nobody, as far as we know. Except the owner, of course, but as I said he's overseas.'

'Right...' Sharon thought for a few moments. 'So where do you keep the keys overnight?'

'On set's with our car keys and the other's in my handbag. Same as at home, overnight we leave the car keys on a coat peg in the hall. John checked. They're still there. But wherever we are we always lock the door at night, and I'm pretty sure we locked it last night, too...'

Sharon nodded and smiled encouragingly. 'Are you quite certain the spare key is still in your handbag?' she asked.

'Oh, well, yes, I *think* so,' Mrs Dawson said. 'I always keep it beside the bed. The handbag, I mean. I can go and check if you like.'

'No Marge,' John Dawson said, rising to his feet. 'Leave that to me. You put the kettle on and make the inspector a cuppa.'

'You're promoting me two grades,' the DC said with a smile. 'I'm just a detective constable. Thank you all the same, but I'm fine.'

It was as if Margaret Dawson hadn't heard her. 'Tea or coffee? We're both having tea, but I can do either.'

'Oh, well... thank you then. Tea with milk but no sugar.'

As Marge wheeled her way into the kitchen, John Dawson returned from the bedroom waving a key ring with two keys. 'Spare keys to the outside door and to the flat,' he said. 'Both here.'

Sharon sighed. 'Right. So if your wife locked up last night, it seems whoever got in must have picked the lock while you were asleep. Do you know if Fallon Towers has got CCTV security?'

'It hasn't. Marge asked about that before she made the booking. But there are bars on all the ground floor windows, including ours, so we thought it would be okay.'

'Your tea, inspector.'

'Oh, thank you Marge. That was quick.' Sharon glanced at her watch just as the carriage clock on the mantelpiece chimed eight times. Then her phone buzzed. 'Oh, I've just had a text update from my DI. He says he expects to be here in about half an hour, all being well. Traffic's always *so* much worse on Fridays. Everybody wants to start work as early as possible so they can get off, especially if they're going away for the weekend.'

Marge smiled and pointed to Sharon's cup. 'Don't let you tea go cold, dear.' Taking a long sip from her own cup she added, 'I never make it very hot.'

Sharon drank her tea quickly. She wanted to get on with the interview. 'That was lovely. Thank you.'

'More refreshing than coffee, we think, don't we John?'

John Dawson nodded and peered at Sharon over the rim of his teacup. 'Thanks, Marge,' he said as he returned his own cup to its saucer. 'I needed that. The tea, I mean, not being burgled.'

Sharon Wallis finished her drink and wiped her forehead with her sleeve, wondering why old people have their living rooms so hot and stuffy. She sat back in the chair and looked at her watch again. Three minutes past eight. 'Such a waste of time…'

'Are you okay, dear?'

Marge Dawson had drawn her wheelchair alongside Sharon and was shaking her arm. 'For a moment I thought you'd fainted. Your eyes were closed.'

Sharon shook her head and looked around the room. John Dawson was still in his chair, but now he was sitting up and looking concerned. 'What did you mean, a waste of time?' he asked.

'Did I say that? Sorry.' Sharon held a hand to her brow. 'Bit of a headache coming on. Nothing serious. I must have lost concentration.'

'John. Get the inspector a drink of water. It's probably much too warm in here for you dear. Since his stroke my husband really feels the cold.'

Sharon nodded and then checked her watch again. Nearly five past eight. The second hand of the mantelpiece clock swept past the twelve. Exactly five past. Another 25 minutes or so before Mike would get there, unless he'd been able to leave earlier than expected or been exceptionally lucky with the traffic.

Barely ten minutes later they heard a car draw up outside Fallon Towers, and John Dawson went to the window. 'It's a police car. Must be your colleague. Maybe the traffic wasn't so bad after all. I'll go and let him in.'

As Detective Inspector Mike Horton entered the sitting room, Sharon was struggling to her feet. She stood unsteadily and stared at him, a look of puzzlement on her face.

The DI grinned. 'Good party last night? Maybe you should have had more water with it.'

Sharon frowned. 'No. I mean no party. It's just… you got here much sooner than I was expecting.'

'Really? Usual snarl ups and queues at every roundabout, plus a couple of prangs, so just the typical Friday morning misery,' the DI replied with a grin. His DC didn't look at all happy. 'What's up, Sharon?'

'Your colleague's got a bit of a headache, that's all,' Marge Dawson said. 'She's been very kind and helpful. I assume you know about our break in?'

The newcomer nodded and turned again towards his junior partner. 'You okay?'

'Yes Mike. I'm fine, really. But I'm not convinced it *was* a break in. It looks as if someone had a key or maybe picked the lock. Tricky, though. It's a five-lever mortice lock.'

'Not the most secure, but by no means a pushover,' Horton muttered. 'Bolts? A chain?'

'No,' Sharon said. 'I was going to discuss all that while waiting for you to arrive. The Dawsons are only renting short term, but in any case I'll be sending them our advice sheet for making homes more secure.'

Horton nodded, sat down and turned to Mrs Dawson. 'We'll need a bit more information about the stuff that's missing. Photographs if you've got any, or at least a description. But first' – he glanced at Sharon – 'my colleague and I need to go and check the other flats and public areas of the building. Lock yourselves in while we're away. Sharon will phone you if for any reason we're going to be more than half an hour. Okay?'

Mrs Dawson nodded. 'Yes, of course. Thank you.'

When the detectives had left, John Dawson returned to his accustomed armchair. 'Okay?'

His wife nodded. 'Now we just wait.'

Faisal Malik appeared surprised but not unduly alarmed when he opened his door and was confronted by two police warrant cards.

'Mr Malik?'

The young man nodded. 'Something wrong?'

'Can we come in please?'

The young man shrugged. 'Sure,' he said. He looked at his watch. 'Excuse the mess, I was going to tidy up. I've got a couple of hours before I leave for work.'

'Did you hear anything unusual during the night, sir?'

'Me? No chance. When I go to sleep I'm dead to the world. Why?'

'It seems there may have been a break in to one of your neighbours' flats. Can you just check your own valuables? Wallet, phone, cameras, that sort of thing.'

Faisal Malik smiled. 'Easy. Wallet and phone are always beside the bed when I'm asleep.' He patted his pockets. 'All okay. Nothing else worth nicking, that's for sure.'

'Okay. That's all for now, sir. Could you let DC Wallis have your mobile number, please? We may need a brief statement from you if anyone is apprehended and charged.'

'Oh. One more thing,' Sharon said. 'Do you know who lives in the other flats?'

Malik knew the names of all of the occupants except the new people in number one.

The couple in flat two and an old man in flat three were just getting up, but they had heard nothing either.

There was no reply from number five, which the detectives now knew belonged to Marie-Claire Rousseau, a retired GP. Her door was still securely locked and a parcel box immediately outside contained an Amazon delivery dated two days ago. 'She must be away,' Horton said. Five and six were for sale and both currently vacant.

'Just the top floor left. Seven, eight and nine. According to Malik seven's been empty for months awaiting refurbished after a water leak. Insurance battle, I'll bet. The Morrison family's in eight and an Irish bloke - Eamon what's 'is name – he's in nine. '

In the lift, Sharon checked her notes. 'According to our friend Faisal, Eamonn McCafferty runs some sort of import-export business.'

'Shit!' Horton yelled as the lift doors parted. The door to flat nine was wide open. 'Mr McCafferty? Police! Anyone at home?'

They found McCafferty in bed. His head was a bloody mess.

Sharon stifled a scream. She reached out to put a finger on the man's neck. 'He's alive, Mike. Out stone cold, though. No sign of a struggle.'

'Don't touch anything, Sharon.' Horton took out his handkerchief and went to place it on the head wound but then thought better of it. 'He's not bleeding badly, so let's leave it to the paramedics.'

Sharon was already making the call.

'About ten minutes they reckon, Mike. McCafferty's damned lucky. A crew just aborted a call from the railway station. False alarm.'

'Okay. Take a few photos, Sharon, but that's all. We need to get forensics in here. If McCafferty dies we're looking at a murder scene. He definitely didn't do that to himself. Look!' Horton was pointing at a blood-stained metal candlestick lying on the floor. 'There might be fingerprints on it. I doubt it, though. If he's got even half a brain the assailant would have been wearing gloves. And probably a mask too, just in case the poor sod heard him and woke up before being clobbered.'

Sharon looked around the bedroom. Apart from the single bed and a bedside cabinet, the room contained only a small wardrobe, a chair across which the man's clothes were draped, and in one corner a large metal safe. The door of the safe was wide open, and it appeared to be empty. Hardly the typical pad of a successful businessman, she thought.

'That's odd, Mike. His wallet's still on the bedside cabinet.'

Horton thought for a few moments. 'You're right, it's *very* odd. This was no opportunist crime. Whatever the intruder was after must have been inside the safe. But how the hell would he have opened it without help from McCafferty?'

'Just like with the Dawsons, the intruder must have had a key to the flat. And known the safe combination.'

'I guess so,' the DI said. 'If McCafferty pulls through we'll need to know who else he gave door keys and his safe combination to. And you know what I think his answer will be?'

'Nobody?'

'Yep. That's my guess too.' The DI frowned and shook his head. 'I can't put my finger on it, but something's not quite right here, Sharon. Anyway, while we're waiting for the ambulance, I'll stay here with McCafferty in case he comes to. You nip down and tell the Dawsons to stay locked in until the crime scene people get here.'

~~~

'No,' Superintendent Ken Wilberforce said. 'The Dawson's haven't lodged a complaint. *I* have. We know why Sharon Wallis's prints were on the Dawson's coffee table and on a teacup cup and a water glass in their lounge. So far we've found nothing else of concern in their flat.'

'Okay,' Horton said. 'So what's the complaint about, then?'

'At first I thought it was just a professional conduct matter. Something we could deal with internally. I realise that DC Wallis was under pressure, but after nearly ten years in CID you can hardly put it down to inexperience. She shouldn't have touched that candlestick. You know that. If the intruder had handled it, her prints may have obliterated crucial forensic evidence.'

'Hang on, sir. I was with her when we found McCafferty. She checked for a pulse, but I'm sure she never touched that candlestick. I was with her all the while she was there. First thing I said was don't touch anything.'

'I'm not doubting you, Mike. I'm sure you didn't see her touch the candlestick, but the fact is Sharon Wallis's prints are on what could so easily have been a murder weapon. I have no choice but to suspend her from duty. I wanted you to know first, and I'd like you to be here when I call her in.'

'I can't believe this is happening,' Horton replied. 'So, were her prints on the safe as well?'

The superintendent shook his head. 'No. It was clean, apart from McCafferty's prints, that is. What a nightmare, poor sod. Perhaps it's just as well he didn't wake up before he was clouted over the head.'

'How's he doing?' Horton asked.

'Severe concussion. A dozen stitches. They're keeping him in overnight for observation. Anyway, for what it's worth he's given us a brief statement. Says he heard nothing, saw nothing. Claims he can't remember what was in the safe. Just papers, he thinks. That I find hard to believe. Something dodgy, perhaps? Anyway, I've got Aileen looking into his background. But about DC Wallis. We've no choice, Mike. You must know that.'

Mike Horton sighed. 'Yes sir. I know. It's just…' He frowned. 'She's a straight as they come, sir. I'm sure there'll be a perfectly simple explanation.'

'I do hope so, Mike.'

The superintendent dialled a number and said, 'Sharon? Could you join Inspector Horton and me in my office please? Yes, now please.'

When Sharon Wallis entered what the team referred to as 'the inner sanctum' her DI and the superintendent were seated behind the desk.

'Take a seat please, Sharon. I'm going to have to ask you a few questions about the break in at Fallon Towers.'

'Something wrong, sir?'

The superintendent frowned. 'I'll ask the questions. At what time did you first enter McCafferty's flat?'

Sharon was puzzled by the wording, but she thought for a moment and then said, 'About ten to eight, sir.'

'By all means check your notes, constable.'

Sharon glanced down at the notebook on her lap. 'Ten minutes to eight.'

The superintendent scribbled something on the pad on his desk. 'And then?'

'Well, I stayed with the Dawsons until Mike arrived – Inspector Horton. That was just gone a quarter past eight. We then checked the five other flats on the ground floor and second floors. They were all secure. Then we took the lift up to the top floor. That would have been about 20 past eight, maybe 25 past. That's when we found McCafferty's door wide open.'

DI Horton stared at Sharon but said nothing as the superintendent stared at a notebook open on his desk. 'According to DI Horton's notes, he arrived at Fallon Towers at 8.35. His SatNav records confirm that. So are you saying that you were in McCafferty's flat some fifteen minutes before your DI joined you?'

'No sir. Something's wrong. DI Horton and I were *together* when we found McCafferty unconscious. Check with the ambulance service, they'll have a record of when I called for emergency-'

Something in the inspector's expression stopped Sharon in her tracks. 'What is it?' she asked.

'We've already checked. You made the emergency call at 8.47. That's nearly 20 minutes later than you are claiming. The question is, what were you doing between 7.50, when you entered the Dawsons' flat, and 8.35 when DI Horton joined you in the flat?'

Sharon felt the flesh crawling on her scalp. What was going on? 'But sir, I've told you. I interviewed the Dawsons in their flat and stayed with them until Mike arrived.' She turned to Horton. 'You know I was with the Dawsons, Mike. Say something, for God's sake.'

The superintendent stepped in before Horton could reply. 'DI Horton has already confirmed that you were in the Dawson's flat when he arrived. But I've now got a sworn statement from the Dawsons who say that after a brief interview you told them to lock themselves in while you checked the other flats in the block. You were away about ten to fifteen minutes, they say.'

'They're lying! I've no idea why, sir, but they are.'

The inspector frowned and looked down at his notes. 'So are the ambulance service lying, too?'

Sharon felt nauseous. She shook her head and instinctively clutched the arms of the chair.

'Okay,' the superintendent said. 'Let's leave the timeline for now. Why did you handle that candlestick, which was clearly the instrument used to beat McCafferty almost to death?'

'I *didn't* sir.' Sharon turned again to her DI. 'You were with me, Mike. You *know* I didn't.'

Horton nodded. 'I've already said that I am pretty sure you didn't touch the candlestick while we were in the room together.'

'Your prints are on the candlestick, Sharon,' the superintendent said. 'Yours and nobody else's. Surely you don't need me to spell out the significance of that. If someone else had wielded that weapon you could have contaminated or even obliterated crucial forensic evidence.'

'What do you mean… *if* someone else had handled it? What am I being accused of? Burglary? Attempted murder? This is ludicrous.' Still terrified, she was now also angry.

'I'll ask you one more time, Constable Wallis. When and why did you handle that candlestick?

Sharon Wallis shook her head. 'I did *not*.'

'Okay. Let's leave that for now. Why have you falsified the time line in your notebook? What were you doing between 8.05 and 8.35?'

Sharon held her head in her hands. 'Honestly, sir. I've told the truth. I haven't done any of those things. Are you… are you going to charge me?'

'No. At least not yet. But I'm far from satisfied with your explanation, or rather your lack of any sort of credible explanation. You're suspended from duty with immediate effect pending further enquiries. Hand over your keys, warrant card, police phone and notebook, and do *not* go back to your desk. I want you to make a full statement detailing what you claim happened between the time you received the call from the duty officer at 7.42 this morning and 9.28 when you and DI Horton left Fallon Towers. DI Townsend and DS Sanchez are waiting for you in interview room 3. Then go home and stay there until we-' A knock at the door the superintendent said, 'Yes?'

'Sorry to interrupt, sir. DI Townsend says you need to see this.'

The superintendent stared at the note he had just been handed. He sighed, looked up at DC Willis and said, 'After your formal interview, we'll arrange for a car will take you home. Your own car is being impounded for further examination.'

'*What*! But why, for God's sake? What do you think is in my car to make that necessary?'

The superintendent scowled. 'An initial check of your car has revealed a pair of pearl earrings matching the description given by Mrs Dawson, and a metal candlestick, the companion to the one found at the scene of the assault. If you could explain in your written statement how those items came into your possession that would be very helpful.'

Sharon Wallis opened her mouth to protest again, but the superintendent raised a hand. 'That's all, constable. I hope there is an innocent explanation for the discrepancies between what we have found so far and what you told me in this initial interview, but until then I'm sorry but you're on gardening leave. Stay away from the station, and on no account go anywhere near Fallon Towers until this matter is resolved. One way or another.'

~~~

'Sorry Mike,' the superintendent said. 'The answer's no. You know the rules. Keep out of it. Karen and Tim are handling it. I'm going to keep you updated because Sharon Willis has been in your team for the past couple of years.'

'Nearly four years, sir,' Horton replied. 'And I appreciate it. But I also know Sharon. I would trust her with my life. Someone else beat up McCafferty and stole whatever was in his safe. If there's anything I can do to help prove her innocence I'll do it…'

'Mike. I'm not jumping to conclusions, I promise you. Sharon Wallis is innocent until proven guilty. We haven't charged her with anything, but so far I have to say the evidence does seem pretty damning.'

'There has to be some other explanation, sir. Maybe if I could interview her-'

'No! And that's final. While I can understand your concern for a team member, you must realise that you could be a crucial witness in a very serious case.'

The DI nodded. 'I know that, Ken.'

'Okay. So, under no circumstances are you to visit DC Wallis. And don't phone her either. If she phones you with questions about the case, don't answer them. That's an order.'

When Mike Horton got back home that evening there were three missed calls on his landline, all from Sharon Wallis and the same message each time. 'Mike, I think I know why my timeline differs from yours. Phone me back, please.'

On his drive home, something else had been bothering Mike Horton. When he went into the Dawson's flat, the look on Sharon's face was one of confusion, not fear. Her hands were shaking and she said she had a headache, but she pulled herself together and seemed genuinely shocked when they found McCafferty unconscious and bloody. If she was putting on an act, it was a bloody good one.

Horton's landline phone rang again and he was sure it would be Sharon. I haven't got caller ID, so no one can blame me for answering, he thought.

'Mike Horton.'

'Mike. It's me, Sharon. We need to talk.'

'I'm sorry, Sharon. I can't tell you anything. The super has expressly forbidden me from discussing the case with you.'

A pause, and then. 'Okay... then just listen. But please don't hang up 'til I'm finished.'

'Okay, I'm listening.'

'First I need a simple yes or no answer, Mike. I know Wilberforce thinks I did it. The robbery, the assault on McCafferty. I'm telling you, I didn't do any of it. Do you believe me?'

This was not an unexpected question. Horton had thought of nothing else since seeing Sharon being frogmarched into the interview room nearly two hours ago. Without a moment's hesitation he replied. 'I believe you, Sharon. Absolutely.'

'Good. Then you need to hear this.' Sharon paused until she heard a grunt of agreement. 'Okay. When I got home I discovered that my watch was nearly twenty minutes slow. All the times I quoted to Wilberforce… they were way out, but only for that reason. I wasn't lying. My watch was lying. At the time I just thought you'd had an easy journey and got to the flat about fifteen minutes earlier than expected.'

'Come off it, Sharon. That would be virtually impossible, even if mine was the only car on the road.'

'I realise that now. The point is, your times are right and my records are all about twenty minutes out. What does that tell you?'

'I'm not supposed to be talking to you about *anything*, Sharon. I'm sorry but-'

'Then don't talk. Just listen. There's only one logical explanation. Unless you believe I'm capable of burglary and attempted murder, that is,'

Another grunt, then, 'Okay…'

Five minutes later, when Sharon had finished, Horton said. 'Stay there, Sharon. I'll be with you in half an hour.'

~~~

Superintendent Wilberforce was scowling. 'I should have been at a lunch meeting half an hour ago. If I've let the Chamber of Commerce down for no good reason I'll have your-'

'I know when, where, how and why McCafferty was beaten up and left for dead.'

'And who by?'

'That's your decision, sir. I just need ten minutes, uninterrupted, to present you with the facts. Please.'

Wilberforce was angry, but the look of determination on Mike Horton's face persuaded him not to pull rank and eject the source of his annoyance. He gave the DI a long hard stare, sat back in his swivel chair and sighed. 'Okay. I'm listening. But this had better be bloody good.'

Horton nodded and began, 'Two conflicting scenarios, sir. Only one of them can make a credible case to present to the CPS.'

The superintendent still looked angry, but he remained silent.

'Scenario one. Sharron Wallis, a cold calculating villain. The case as presented by Townsend and Sanchez.

'An officer with a ten-year impeccable record is called to a break in. She briefly interviews the victims, and when their backs are turned she steals two old chrome-plated candlesticks and a pair of fake pearl earrings. Total hoard unlikely to fetch more than twenty quid. On the pretext of checking other flats she goes to the top floor, quickly picks a five-lever mortice lock, creeps in and bashes the sleeping occupant over the head, nearly killing him. Then she works out a way of opening a very expensive safe containing nothing but a few innocuous documents. She thoroughly wipes the safe clean of any of her fingerprints while somehow avoiding wiping off McCafferty's prints, but she leaves behind the incriminating bloody candlestick with her own fingerprints on it. She goes out to her car and dumps the stolen earrings and the other candlestick on the back seat, in plain sight stupidly, rather than in the boot. But remembering to wipe her fingerprints off. She then returns to the ground-floor flat to await my arrival, meanwhile filling in her notebook without realising that the duty officer, the ambulance service and I will all have time records that contradict hers. Now how stupid is that?'

The look of confusion on Wilberforce's face allowed Horton to move on uninterrupted.

'Scenario two. Sharon Willis, victim. The case as presented by me.'

Ken Wilberforce was now sitting bolt upright. 'Go on…'

'Sharon arrives at Fallon Towers at 7.50, as recorded in her notebook. She is shown around the Dawson's flat and then begins interviewing them about their reported break in. Hearing that it will be about half an hour before I can join her, she accepts a cup of tea. Her tea is laced with something nasty. Ambien, Rohypnol, Ketamine, something of the sort… we'll find out. So, Sharon's out of it for ten to fifteen minutes, during which time John Dawson, wearing gloves, wraps Sharon's hand – actually the left hand, although Sharon is right handed - around the top of the candlestick to leave her prints on it. He then goes up and gets into McCafferty's room using a key, and he bludgeons the poor sod senseless. He already knows the safe combination, my guess is through an accomplice, and he removes the valuables. Then he dumps the earrings and spare candlestick in Sharon's car and returns to the flat. The Dawsons adjust Sharon's watch and their mantelpiece clock to show that she's been out of it for no more than a minute or two, and they shake her awake and give her a drink of water. She's still a bit vague when I arrive at 8.37. So what-'

Wilberforce could hold it in no longer.

'Any evidence for this incredible second scenario, as you call it?'

'How about this?' Horton said. 'Yesterday morning when one of my DCs and I arrested them at Manchester Airport, the Dawsons were about to board a flight to Panama City. Thereafter, well… who knows? Currently they're being held in detentions cells one and four, so they can't communicate with each other. But before you say anything, sir, I think you'll be interested in what we found in their checked luggage.' Horton held up a bottle of Malvern Water. 'They had a sealed package containing six of these in their suitcase.'

'Have you gone barking mad?' the superintendent yelled, leaping to his feet and spilling the remains of his coffee over the desk. 'Even I know that Malvern Water went out of production years ago. So what's the big deal?'

'They're fakes,' Horton snapped back. 'Watch, and learn.' He walked over to the waste paper bin, broke the seal on the bottle and poured its contents through a handkerchief and into the bin. 'Voila!'

The superintendent stared at more than a dozen glass-like beads that stood out against the damp blue background. 'Are they what I think they are?'

Horton nodded. 'Uncut diamonds. Invisible in water. I've already shown one set to an expert. They're genuine all right. None less than ten and some more than thirty carats. He reckons that even on the black market the whole consignment's got to be worth at least four million quid. Possibly two or three times that.'

'And they belonged to McCafferty?'

Horton shook his head. 'No way. He's just a minion. A post box for an international smuggling ring. Knowing a bit about how these people operate, I'm pretty sure McCafferty won't have a clue what's in the packages he collects, where they come from or their final destination. But the Dawsons – well, let's carry on calling them that for now – they found out, and they planned the interception down to the very last detail. Whoever responded to their 999 call would have become a convenient smokescreen. The Dawsons just needed to mislead us for a couple of days and they would have been clear away. They or their associates will have had an outlet ready and waiting. Probably not Antwerp. More likely someone in the Panama Diamond Exchange. Go about it the right way and there's a good chance we can get the Dawsons to sing in return for shorter sentences. We could get lucky and land some really big fish.'

'Jesus!' Superintendent Ken Wilberforce sank back into his chair and thought for a moment. 'Bloody well done, Mike. You're a genius!'

'No me. One of our DCs worked it all out. Would you like me to send the genius in now, sir?'

'Oh, yes. Yes, do that, Mike.'

'Good morning, sir.'

Superintendent Ken Wilberforce looked up from his notes and did a double take. His jaw dropped open but no words emerged.

'Are you okay, sir?'

'Yes. Er, yes, Sharon. Sit down. Please. I think I owe you-'

'A promotion, sir? I thought you'd never ask.'

-oo0oo-

15 Melting Pot

"The Supreme Court has ruled that disgraced Detective Sergeant Edwin Blunden's life support system should now be switched off. Blunden, who has spent the past eighteen months in a coma following a head-on collision with a car carrying supporters to the UK Snooker Championships, was awaiting trial on drug-running charges. Already convicted of falsifying police records, Blunden would have faced a life sentence if found guilty of these drugs offences. The detective was purportedly pursuing drugs baron Heinz Wortenberger; however, a Sunday Times investigation revealed compelling evidence that Blunden was in fact Wortenberger. The case will not now come to trial. BBC Radio Four News.

"Now for sport, and over to The Crucible in Sheffield, where the World Snooker Championships are approaching a nail-biting climax..."

~~~

The door to the dimly-lit room burst open. 'I'm looking for a Heinz Wortenberger.'

The bald man crouched over the snooker table miscued, sighed and half turned towards the intruder. 'Did you *have* to do that? I was on for a personal best there, mate.' He did not look happy. His lanky partner was grinning broadly.

'Snooker,' the newcomer groaned. 'It's the one spectator sport that bores me to death. My idea of purgatory. I'd rather watch paint dry.'

The taller snooker player frowned and looked pensive. 'Heinz Wortenberger, you say... can't say for sure, 'cos I've never been there, but you could try the brimstone bar, next door.' He waved vaguely in the direction of a yellow glow seeping through an arched doorway. 'Rumour has it they do all sorts of weird stuff there. Who knows? Maybe even food.'

The newcomer reached into his inside pocket and held up a warrant card.

'Oops, how can we help you constable,' the tall man said.

'I'm not a constable.'

The shorter man shook his head and pointed an accusing finger. 'Serious offence, that... impersonating a police officer. Not to mention putting me off when I was only 97 short of a maximum break.'

The policeman thrust his warrant card at the speaker's face. 'See that? It says *Sergeant* Blundel, and I have reason to believe that someone on these premises is implicated in criminal activities. Of course, if you'd rather answer my questions down at the station...'

The shorter player leant on his snooker cue. 'That might prove a tad difficult. Anyway, questions like what, for example?'

Sergeant Blundel stroked his chin. 'Casting my mind back to what I was told as a trainee, I'm pretty sure that *questioning suspects* means that *I* ask the questions and you, the *suspects*, are expected to answer. Or do you know otherwise? If not, shall we try it my way?'

The snooker players stared at each another, nodded, grinned, shook their heads and shrugged, all in synchrony, before turning to face their inquisitor. '*No*,' the tousle-haired tall man said.

'Then I'll have to caution you. You are not obliged to say-'

'And *yes*,' the shorter, red-faced resident interjected.

Blundel frowned. 'What the hell do you think you're playing at?' His eyes narrowed, 'Have you two been taking something?'

'Snooker. And nothing. No means no, we don't know what rookie cops are taught. And yes means yes, we'll try it your way. But if you're accusing us of theft you're barking up the wrong tree.'

Blundel was getting extremely hot under the collar. 'Enough!' he growled. 'I need your names and addresses.'

'We're Bill and Ben Potts,' Bill or Ben said.

'Oh, *really*?' Blunden was sneering now. 'Well, I'm warning you… if I find so much as a Little Weed here I'll charge you with possession.'

'Possession? You've definitely come to the right place for that, mate.' It might have been Bill or Ben talking, or possibly both at once.

'So… Permanent address, including post code.'

'How the hell would we know the infernal post code? We're here now, and we're not going anywhere. What more do you need?'

'Where do you actually *live*? And for that matter where *is* little weed?'

Bill, the red-faced man, frowned. 'We don't *live* anywhere. This is our *permanent* abode. And what little weed we may have had went up in smoke the moment we got here.'

'Permanently here,' Ben echoed. 'Arrived by car, together. Same day, same time, same place. *Boom!*'

'That's utter gibberish. Driving licences, *now!*'

The two men handed over their driving licences, which Sergeant Blunden held side by side. 'Hmm… William Potts… Benjamin Potts… same date of birth… I'm sorry, but you don't look at all like twins.'

'We're not,' the tall Mr Potts said. 'I was an only child. My Uncle Tim and Auntie Connie had twins, though. Connie said she found it much easier to tell them apart once they had grown up.'

Intrigued, the sergeant couldn't resist asking, 'How come?'

'Well, Jessica had curly blonde hair and her brother was completely bald by the age of thirty, weren't you Bill?'

Bill sighed, Ben laughed, and Sergeant Blundel blushed before jotting something down in his notebook.

'So… you're cousins, I take it?'

'We're cousins,' the two men said, almost together.

Bill was frowning. 'You said *I take it*, although you didn't say what. But a few moments ago you seemed to be accusing *us* of taking something, and again you didn't say what. Were you *really* a policeman?'

'*Still* a policeman,' Blundel snapped. 'You people need to understand what that means.'

'We may not be quick,' Ben replied, 'but like everybody here we really do understand what still means.'

'And *you* need to understand that we've got to get on with our game,' Bill added. 'We can talk to you again in the interval, if you like.'

'And when *will* that be?' Blundel demanded, curiosity barely masking his anger.

'Well, we're only in the early stages of the tournament,' Bill replied, 'so the matches are relatively short. Best of a million frames.'

'With a replay if we're tied at half a million each,' Ben added. 'We're currently on four thousand one hundred and three frames apiece, so-'

'Hell!' Blundel yelled. 'I'll be stuck here forever!'

'You're right,' Bill and Ben said in perfect harmony. Blundel groaned and blundered off through the side door into a darkened room where a long-haired lanky man crouched over the snooker table miscued, sighed and half turned towards the intruder.

'Did you *have* to barge in like that, mate? I'd have won the frame and levelled the match if I'd potted that black.' He did not look happy. His bald partner wore a devilish grin.

-oo0oo-

16 Don't Tell the Children

'Your dad thinks I'm in my second childhood,' Marion Watson said. 'Maybe he's right, but I hope you don't think I've lost the plot completely, my dear.'

'Of course you haven't, gran,' Mandy said, her earnest seven-year-old eyes staring up at her grandmother. She was so glad that they now lived next door to Granny Watson. They had moved in less than a week ago, and Mandy had no idea where her gran's plot was, but she decided it couldn't be important. 'I think you're very grown up and the cleverest person in the whole world. And we all love you. Mum, dad and me. Me, especially.'

'Thank you, Mandy. It's always nice to be told you're loved, and so much nicer when it's said by someone you love.'

Mandy Watson frowned. 'Did dad say *why* he though you weren't grown up?'

'Oh, it's not… well, I suppose it's because I keep telling him that your granddad could do magic with his paint brushes.' The peering eyes widened, prompting the old lady to go on. 'A long time ago, when granddad got too ill to run the farm, we moved here, to The Gables. Granddad turned his hobby into his work. He did hundreds of paintings and sold them in the shop next door. They flew off the shelves almost as soon as the paint was dry. There's one of granddad's pictures on your kitchen wall, and I think Uncle Harold's still got one in his attic. The poppies…' – the old lady waved at a picture on the fire screen - 'well… they're all I've got to show you.'

'Flew off the shelves? That's magic.' Mandy swivelled round and looked at the poppies. 'They're very beautiful. Just like real, but better somehow. Three flowers open and… six more in bud. Why didn't he paint more of them open?'

'It's how they were when he painted this picture. Your granddad's paintings were always true to life.'

~~~

'Three more of Granny's poppies have opened since yesterday, and two of the old ones have lost their petals and have now got seed heads,' Mandy said as she sat down for dinner.

'In November? I don't think so, Mandy love. Poppies are summer flowers.'

'In granddad's magic painting, not in the garden.'

'Of course,' Paul Watson said with a sigh and a shrug of the shoulders. 'Now, Mandy… you haven't forgotten that Uncle Harold is coming over on Sunday. He'll want to know what you've been up to at school. He always asks.'

~~~

'Hello granny. I'm back. You okay?' Mandy climbed carefully onto the welcoming lap and gave her grandmother a hug.

'Much better now you're back from school, my dear.'

Mandy smiled and turned to admire the poppies. 'Oh look! Three flowers open today, and six more in bud… again.'

'You're nearly seven. Three months before your granddad died, when your dad and Uncle Harold were nine years old, he painted this fire screen for my Fortieth birthday. He made me promise not to tell our twins how the magic works. Not unless they ask, he said. In all these years your dad and Uncle Harold have never even noticed the magic. But you did.'

'Wow! So now are you going to tell me how it works?'

'Better than that, Mandy. I'm going to *show* you how it works. Turn the fire screen round, so we can see how many poppies are in flower on the other side.'

17 No Going Back

Keen to please, IT specialist Zoe Zuhra Zakari never complains when given dross and trivia to deal with at work. As a result it's assumed that is what she wants, and so she gets more and more of this unrewarding work, making it impossible to stand out from the crowd. Instead, she stands back. Lukewarm invitations to after-work social activities are few and far between, mainly, she knows, because her lukewarm responses suggest she would prefer not to be asked. Which is true. And in recent years she hasn't been asked at all. Until now.

Suddenly she is no longer 'Zoe who? Oh, yes… *that* Zoe. Nice girl but a bit… well, you know.'

Over the years she hears such remarks many times and wonders what the 'you know' is meant to imply. Quiet? Stand-offish? Stuck up? Or maybe boring. Yes, probably boring, she concludes. Her sleepy initials can't help. ZZZ. She has her Ghanaian parents to thank for that. And so, not wanting to bore anyone, she keeps herself to herself as much as possible. But when on her own Zoe is never bored. She finds *everything* interesting – history, nature, politics, sport, world cultures and religions, art and literature, music and dance, medical science and astronomy. She has never been actively involved in any of these. But interested? A great big *Yes*. Zoe has boned up on all this and more, listening to podcasts as she wanders at weekends in woodlands and waysides or mooches about on mountains and moorlands; reading on workday evenings or tuning in to documentaries, dramas, sci-fi and horror movies; filtering out the key facts, and committing them all to memory. Why? Not merely because she *can*, but because it is something that she *excels* at. Zoe's brain is a super-thirsty information sponge with rapid recall that would have made her a formidable Mastermind contestant. Except that Zoe would never dream of using her talent to impress (or depress) others. Not intentionally. Only bores do that. In fact she rarely needs to access all this knowledge other than to work out exactly where new chunks of learning need to be lodged.

Until she finds a purpose.

Zoe has heard people complain of boredom, but it is never boredom with who they are. Either they are bored with what they have to *do,* or more often with who they do it *with* - especially those who have partners or spouses.

Boredom is one of the few things that Zoe Zakari does not understand, and for that reason she makes a special study of it. She produces case studies to support her conclusions about the causes and cures of this pernicious affliction that she fears is becoming pandemic.

People who can't cope with being alone say they are lonely. Unless they have either a screen to peer at – which they called 'being entertained' – or someone else to blame for the way they feel – which they call 'being bored' – they tell themselves they feel unvalued, unloved, depressed, even suicidal. Bored to death.

And when after much study Zoe understands boredom, albeit without ever having experienced it, she produces an app, *No Going Back*, dedicated to the banishment of boredom.

Unlike so many clever apps that do lots of difficult things, *No Going Back* is smart; it does just one thing. Zoe's app turns a few simple (to ask!) questions inside out in a way that makes the user feel much smarter than the app. Smart move!

First, the *No Going Back* app offers the user a wide range of descriptive terms – kind, cruel, generous, selfish, timid, daring, jocular, serious and so on - and asks them to select via tick boxes those that best describe the kind of person they most hate to be alone with – their worst nightmare of a bore. Users can even add descriptive terms of their own (but no expletives, please). The app always thanks users for helping to improve its usefulness. Another smart move.

Next the user is asked to select from the same range of terms, again adding others if they wish, to describe the kind of person they would like to be with long term.

Finally the *No Going Back* app invites the user to select from the same range (but this time they *can't* add any new ones) the terms that best describe themselves. At this stage users invariably want to go back and either add in new terms or change some of their earlier selections. That is when they find that the app is so dumb there's no way of going back – they've had their one and only shot at it!

And then Zoe's avatar appears in the app and says, *"That's very interesting. I'm not real, but what I've learned from you is real:*

- *In real life there really is no going back.*

- *I can't change other people, but I **can** change myself.*

- *If I'm lonely it's because I don't like the person I am alone with – myself. To fix that I **must** change myself.*

- *When I find someone boring it's because they haven't shown any real interest in me. I can fix that by taking a real interest in **them**.*

Thank you for your help. If you think other people would benefit from learning what you've taught me, please tell them about the new, improved No Going Back app."

And they do. Zoe's app has ten users on its launch day, for which she earns £1. There are 100 users the next day and ten million by the end of the week.

Inevitably with such a meteoric tech success, Zoe is inundated with requests to '…tell our readers/listeners/viewers what prompted you to produce the *No Going Back* app and what it all really means.' Zoe always demurs, with, 'I prefer to let the *No Going Back* app speaks for itself.'

The next question is equally predictable: 'So how will this success and the celebrity and wealth it brings change your life, Zoe?'

'It won't,' she replies. 'But *I* can. If I want to.'

-ooOoo-

18 Magic

'Remember what we agreed, Becky,' John Waldron told his seven-year-old daughter after Saturday breakfast. 'Granddad gets a very small pension. He can't afford to give you money every time he visits. You'll get a pound from us when you help wash the car or weed the garden, but on the strict understanding you don't accept any more money from granddad. Except for birthdays and Christmas, of course.'

'*Dad!* I really *do* understand. Oh, look! Here he comes now.'

~~~

'How do you do that?' Becky asked, staring at the shiny new £1 coin that her grandfather had just magicked from behind her ear - something he'd done many times before when they'd looked after each other while mum took dad for his weekly hospital treatment.

'It's magic, Becky,' the old man said. 'What else *could* it be?'

'But if you can make money without having to work like other people do… well, that's not really fair, is it?'

The look of concern on the youngster's face made Peter Waldron wish they had opted for a walk, despite the frost and a gusting north wind. He placed the coin on the table, king's head uppermost. 'Well, before I retired I *did* have to work for a living, Becky love.' Her frown had faded, but he sensed that another tricky question was coming.

'Could you magic me a telescope, granddad? It's what I'm saving up my pocket money for.'

The old man stifled a sigh of relief, thinking that he was now off the hook. 'My kind of magic can't *make* things, Becky,' he said. 'It just makes things *move*.'

'I already know how to move the money I've earned. Dad paid me a pound yesterday for helping him clean the car. I think it might be hiding behind my other ear. Can you magic it out, please?'

Having no coins other than the one now on the table, the old man felt trapped. He tried to distract his granddaughter with a gesture. 'Look, Becky! The daffodils on the front lawn are just coming out.'

Without averting her gaze the girl replied, 'They're crocuses, granddad.'

Peering over the sill of the bay window, Peter Waldron could see that the youngster was right: a clump of yellow crocuses brightened one corner of the front lawn, their showy heads shuddering in the stiff breeze. 'Silly me! So they are.' He turned back to the table. The coin had gone. Arms still folded, the girl was staring at him expectantly.

'Becky… did you take the pound coin?'

'Maybe it's jumped back behind my ear. Can you magic it out again, granddad?'

Now Peter Waldron was totally stumped. He went through the motions of reaching behind the girl's ears and then said, 'No, it's definitely not there. Do *you* know where it is?'

'Have you magicked it into one of your pockets?' she asked, an innocent, enquiring face upturned towards him. 'That would be naughty!'

The old man checked his trouser pockets. 'Not there either,' he said.

'No cheating. Jacket pockets, too.'

And there was the £1 coin. With a growing feeling of unease, Peter Waldron held it up for his granddaughter to see and then placed it on the table.

The girl was still frowning. 'It isn't the pound you magicked for me, Granddad. This one's got the *queen* on it.'

'Good grief!' Peter Waldron stared in disbelief at the coin on the table. His granddaughter's arms were still folded across her chest, and she looked as puzzled as he felt. He checked all his pockets again carefully pulling out the linings to make absolutely certain they were empty. 'Nothing there,' he said.

The girl unfolded her hands and pointed at the centre of the table. 'Wow! You really are a magician, granddad.' The coin with the queen's head was back on the table. Beside it was the king's coin. 'You've turned a pound into two pounds,' the girl said excitedly. 'Let's share it, one each. I can't wait to tell mummy. She says there's no such thing as magic.'

~~~

'What did you and granddad get up to while we were away, Becky? I hope you remembered your promise about pocket money.'

Becky nodded and smiled. 'Granddad's still got all his pocket money. He says next week he wants me to show him how to do *my* kind of magic.'

'*You* can do magic?' he asked.

'Not real magic like granddad's. While he was waving you off I put my car-washing pound into his jacket pocket. I've still got *my* pound, except thanks to granddad's magic it's now a shiny new one with a picture of the king on it.'

The innocent face upturned towards him gave away nothing. A budding magician? John Waldron mused. Or an accountant? Maybe both. Only time and Becky will tell.

-ooOoo-

19 Mark of Respect

Even with the hood of her raincoat pulled up, Beatrice Atherton felt cold. The jovial weatherman had forecast blustery winds and occasional showers. No mention of hailstorms, though. Coming after several calm sunny days, lots of folk would have been caught out by this sudden change in mid-May weather. She paused, wondering whether to turn back. Then she remembered: outside the school, just round the next bend, there was a bus shelter where she could sit it out until the worst of the storm had passed.

Beatrice had just set off again when a cry of pain stopped her in her tracks. As she turned, a bucket hat bowled past, gathering speed and hailstones *en route*.

'My hat!' a grey-haired woman groaned. She was on all fours and struggling to get upright. Beatrice called out, 'Wait! Let me help you up.' But by the time Beatrice reached her the unfortunate woman was on her feet and dabbing a tissue at blood that was running down from both knees, her tights now in tatters. She was shaking. Whether that was from the shock of falling or the biting wind sweeping the old dear's hair across her face Beatrice couldn't tell.

'Here... I've got a nice clean hankie,' Beatrice said. 'Let me take a look at those cuts... no, only grazed. You're going to have some nasty bruises, and it's likely you'll be feeling stiff and sore tomorrow. We need to go somewhere warm and get those knees cleaned up properly.'

'You're very kind. Thank you. But I need my hat.'

'Can you walk?' The old lady nodded. 'But my hat-'

'Your hat's not going to get away,' Beatrice assured her. 'It's stuck in the hedge over by the letterbox. Let's go that way. There's a bus shelter, and I can phone for a taxi if you like.'

'No taxi,' the woman said hurriedly. She grasped Beatrice's arm and they set off, the old woman hobbling awkwardly. 'I'll be okay, really.'

By the time they arrived at the bus shelter, the hail had stopped and the sun was finding patches of blue sky between the scurrying clouds. Beatrice went back and collected the hat, now half full of hailstones. 'If a cold compress would help, we've got just the thing,' she said with a smile.

The woman grabbed the hat and stared into it before tipping a pile of ice onto the pavement. She laughed nervously. Beatrice began to giggle, but she stopped suddenly when the old lady put the hat on.

'That won't do you any good at all, dear,' Beatrice said. 'It's freezing cold and soaking wet, inside and out.'

The old woman parted her hair and peered at her rescuer. Her jaw dropped. 'Beat- er, Beatrice, isn't it? The Bomb Squad… primary school?'

'Oh yes. B-O-M-B. Brenda, Olive, Mandy, Beatrice. So you must be Olive, or… *Mandy*?'

'I'm Brenda. Mandy emigrated to Austria… or was it Australia? Anyway, that was years ago. Olive's still around. We're not in touch now, but I know she's got big house on Basset Drive. They were just being built when we were at school, remember? Huge gardens, swimming pool and tennis courts, all locked away behind big iron gates. We used to call it Millionaire's Row.'

Beatrice was still struggling to come to terms with the fact that the scruffily-dressed shambling woman beside her could only be in her late fifties. She had guessed mid to late seventies. 'Of course! Yes, very posh. So… Brenda. Lovely to meet again after all these years.'

'Not like this, it isn't,' Brenda said. 'I must look a dreadful mess.' She stopped and checked her knees. 'Bleeding's nearly stopped. I'll be fine now, thanks.'

'Look,' Beatrice said. 'If you're not in a rush to go anywhere, why don't we get a coffee and give those knees a proper wash? Can't be too careful with open wounds, even small ones. We're only a few minutes from The Roundabout Café.'

'Oh, I know the place you mean. It's where our mum's used to wait for us.' Brenda paused. 'No, sorry… I can't. Didn't bring any money with me. Only came out for a breath of fresh air.'

'I think I can stretch to a couple of coffees with an old friend,' Beatrice said as they ambled on slowly.

'*Friend?* We hardly spoke once we got to secondary school. That wasn't your fault, though.'

They were outside the café now, and Beatrice held the door open. 'Black or white, with our without? Or maybe you'd prefer a cappuccino.'

'Just a white coffee, no sugar,' Brenda replied. 'And thanks again, Beatrice. I'll nip into the loo. Try and tidy myself up a bit.'

When Brenda reappeared, still wearing the soggy hat, her knees were clean and no longer bleeding. Beatrice had thoughtfully chosen a table beside an electric radiator, which although now turned off was still warm.

'Pop your hat on the rad,' Beatrice suggested. 'It'll be warm and most likely dry by the time we leave. Coffee's on the way.'

Brenda appeared apprehensive as she sat down, removed her hat and placed it on a corner of the radiator. Shoulder-length grey hair hung down limply not only at the back and sides of her head but also in front of her face. Carefully pushing hair to one side to expose a triangle of forehead and one eye, she glanced nervously at Beatrice but said nothing.

'Oh dear,' Beatrice said. 'I hadn't realised you'd hit your head when you fell. There's blood-'

'No. It… It's a bloody tattoo, that's all.'

'Oops!' Beatrice said. 'I'm sorry.' Brenda remained silent, and after a few moments Beatrice added, 'I didn't mean any disrespect, Brenda. It's just that I've never even considered getting tattooed. No need. I was born with one. An almost complete map of Wales on my face.' She turned her left cheek towards Brenda, who glanced only briefly at the purple birthmark spanning much of Beatrice's forehead, cheek and chin. The North Wales Coast, Anglesey and the Lleyn Peninsula were just visible through a neat auburn fringe, while the concave sweep of Cardigan Bay skirted her eye and nose. Pembrokeshire and a somewhat elongated Gower Peninsula nestled below her mouth.

'I remember,' Brenda said in little more than a whisper.

Beatrice smiled. 'I got teased about it at school, but I never let that bother me.'

'Really?' A tear ran down from the corner of Brenda's eye. 'Oh, Beatrice… If only I'd known that.'

Beatrice gave her a puzzled look. 'Of *course* it didn't matter. It's part of who I *am*. Some people have receding chins, beaked noses, sticky-out ears, freckles. We're all different. Rather than ridicule them, we should respect those differences. I don't think someone's true worth is anything to do with what they look like. Or what they own. What they do and how they treat other people are far more important. Don't you agree?'

Brenda stared at her hands. She nodded several times but made no reply. Two more big tears splashed onto the table.

Beatrice had never pretended to be anything she wasn't. She was content with who she was, what she did, where she lived. Being well groomed and wearing clothes she felt comfortable in mattered to her, but they had never been major issues in her life. She loved her family, and she kept in touch with the friends she had made over the years as she had moved around for work reasons. Now, recently retired, she was back in her home town, with her folks just a ten-minute walk away – a walk that took her past the secondary school where she had met her childhood sweetheart Andy Atherton, now her husband. She had been Beatrice Ferris then, academically bright and pretty good at sports too. But her real passion had always been the natural world, something she got from her mother. None of the other girls in her class had the slightest interest in nature study, and by fifth form their only focus seemed to be boys. Andy Atherton was too quiet and studious to be on their target list, despite his brilliance at tennis and playing centre forward for the school first team. Beatrice enjoyed his company, though. They went for long walks together looking for rare wildflowers. They talked about the birds and the bees, but that was all… until one day as he was helping her over a steep grassy bank they fell down, laughing. And then he kissed her. After that, they were always together, through university, and then setting up their guided wildlife tours business. Somehow surviving the various recessions and economic crises, they had put money into a pension pot during the good times and paid off the mortgage before reaching forty.

Brenda sniffed, rubbed her eyes and then broke the silence. 'Olive said your disfigurement would put boys off the rest of us. She said we should call you Beetroot Face to make you want to leave the gang. She was so cruel to you. And we were, too. I knew it was wrong, but I didn't speak up. Neither did Mandy. I've felt so ashamed of myself ever since, and it serves me right.'

'You really shouldn't have,' Beatrice said. 'I was never much of a gang girl, and I certainly wouldn't have been interested in any boy who thought my birthmark was a disfigurement.'

Brenda was shaking her head. 'We cut you out,' she said. 'Instead of B-O-M-B - the Bomb Squad - we became M-O-B, Mandy, Olivia, Brenda. The Mob. And we behaved like mobsters. We really did. No more tennis, no countryside walks and picnics together. Just chasing after boys… well, to be honest doing whatever it took and wearing as little as it took to get them to chase after us.' Brenda was in full flow now, unstoppable, as though a dam had been breached and a reservoir of regrets had to be drained. 'We used to hang around pubs and clubs, like gangsters molls. Needless to say the kinds of boys we met were either well on the way to becoming gangsters or already fully qualified and with criminal records to prove it. Like bloody Barrie Greenway! Four years older than me, he was, with a great big Triumph Bonneville and a black crash helmet covered in snakes and lizards. And, as I realised far too late, bugger all between his ears except a cruel streak and an insatiable sex drive. He got me totally sloshed one day and sweet talked me into getting this ghastly tattoo. Said it would turn him on and make sure we were tied together forever.'

Brenda parted her hair to reveal a forehead tattooed with a tangle of snakes biting the heads off lizards, below which were the words "*Barrie's Bird*" in Gothic lettering. 'Snakes butchering lizards on both cheeks, too,' she said. 'A right bloody mess.'

'Wow!' Beatrice said. 'And… did it work? I mean, with Barrie-'

'Did it hell! My folks were furious, of course. Next night I went to where me and Barrie used to meet, and he never turned up. It was a fortnight before I saw the bastard again. He'd been avoiding me, obviously. When he saw me he burst out laughing. I said, "What's your problem, Barrie?" and he said, "It's *your* problem, Bee, not mine." He always called me Bee. Then he said, "That makes six, now. Six stupid birds with that tattoo on their ugly mugs." Then a girl wearing leathers and a pink crash helmet came out of the pub and they roared off together on his motorbike.'

'Oh, how awful,' Beatrice said. 'So what did you do?'

'What the hell *could* I do? But I can tell you one thing for sure. Back in the '80s a face full of bloody tattoos like this didn't do a lot for a girl's job prospects. Another woman I met who'd had her face and neck tattooed went and paid to have them removed. The scarring she was left with was a bloody sight worse than any tattoo. Of course, they take them off with lasers nowadays, but this lot? It would cost me thousands that I simply ain't got. And anyway, it's too late now. There's no point.'

'But… what about work?' Beatrice asked.

'Well, eventually I got a job in a betting office. Lousy pay, but some security at least. There's always gonna be gamblers. And gangsters. Like the lying bastard who gave me the job. Within ten years he owned a chain of betting offices and did loads of other shady stuff on the side.'

Beatrice stared in horror at her re-found friend. 'Don't tell me. Let me guess… Barrie Greenway?'

Brenda nodded and grinned. 'Anyway, I got my own back on the smarmy sod. I shopped him. He got seven years for fraud and extortion. What goes around comes around.'

Beatrice shook her head as she considered that sweeping generalisation. 'You really think so?'

Brenda was unfazed and ploughed on, 'Oh, yes. Barrie got ill and died in prison. Lucky for his wife he'd made the betting-shop business over to her. For tax reasons he told me, but I wasn't fooled. It was just a cover for his other dodgy dealings. She's rolling in it now, of course, and well rid of that evil bugger.'

The waitress came to take away the cups.

'I s'pose we'd better be going,' Brenda said, reaching for her hat. 'A shame, though, I wanted to ask about you. About *your* life and…'

'Next time,' Beatrice said, and Brenda smiled. 'Oh, thank you! I'm really grateful, Beatrice. Not just for the coffee, but-'

Beatrice settled the bill and, as they headed for the door, she said, 'Just one more thing, Brenda. Do you know what Olive did after leaving school?'

'Oh, I thought I told you. She's still running the chain of betting offices.'

-ooOoo-

20 On Reflection

Daniel Dee carries a mug of black coffee through from his tiny kitchen-diner into the hallway. He can hear rain battering against the front door. February fill dyke. Still, he has a month in sunny Barbados to look forward to in March. He pauses in front of a small oval mirror and smiles, and the handsome face with the neatly trimmed moustache and goatee beard smiles back at him. Bloody good for my age, he tells himself as he heads up stairs and slumps into the armchair beside his single bed. Maturity spiced with an infectious air of exciting youthfulness. That's me.

In Daniel's line of business appearances are everything. What matters is not what you are but what you appear to be; not what you do but what you can claim the credit for. He also knows that credibility is about belief not truth. His business? Offering help to people who yearn to earn without having to toil or learn, making it sound so simple to achieve… but only if they invest in his expert advice. Daniel Dee sells the dream of gain without pain, but his own wealth comes not from helping others but from helping himself to the wealth of others. He takes money, delivers an incomprehensibly complex and meaningless set of step-by-step instructions, and then moves on… on to the next temporary abode, and on to the next simple sucker. He owns a villa in Barbados, where he has stashed away more than enough money to be able to retire. Not yet though… he still relishes the challenge, the excitement. And he's smart, in a crafty kind of way. What he does isn't actually illegal. Not quite.

Something about the image in the mirror is niggling Daniel, prompting him to reflect. Yes, it's all about image, he muses. As he sips his coffee he looks back to the start of his non-working life, to what his mother used to call shirking. Silly old cow could only understand hard graft. Graft or craft? Even thirty years ago he had not found it a difficult decision. He makes loads of money as an antisocial influencer. It's never bothered him that he also makes enemies. He knows that the key to success in this game lies in keeping your enemies distant and your friends non-existent. Daniel Dee makes sure he knows who his enemies are and where they live, but never vice versa. Friends? Who needs them? As long as you've got loads of money, you can buy whatever else you want.

But then, I'm smart, he thinks. Not like the rest of the family. David and Daphne Dee, so dull they couldn't see any further up the alphabet, naming their twins Daniel and Darren. All the dees. Da de da de da de da. Daniel chuckles as he recalls some of the pranks he got up to, where he had all the fun and dopey Darren got the blame. Darren Dee... always mother's pet. 'Your brother's always so kind and helpful,' she would say, time after time like a broken gramophone record. 'Why don't you follow his example, Daniel?'

And what good would that have done him? It hadn't got his twin brother very far. Backstreet bicycle repair man with a one-bed attic flat, an overdraft *and* a mortgage. At least, that was all he amounted to last time they'd met. That was when Darren had tried to get him to pay half the cost of a headstone for their father's grave. He'd shelled out fifty quid and told his brother that was all he could afford. He had a meeting arranged with a new client on the afternoon of the funeral, so whether his brother had actually paid for a headstone he did not know. Or care particularly. Certainly no one had consulted *him* over an inscription.

What's brought all this on? He wonders. A glance in the mirror? Mirrors are supposed to show the here and now, not to invoke memories. He shook himself out of his pointless reverie. Time to look forward. He has moved in to a new den and was moving on to a new sucker. Now it's time to get down to business.

But the doorbell intervenes.

'Damn,' he mutters to himself. And then annoyance gives way to unease. Nobody but the landlady knows he is here. She lives next door, but why would she need to see him? He has paid her a month's rent in advance, cash in hand, even though he has no intention of staying there more than a week to ten days.

Unease turns to alarm when he opens the door to find his twin brother standing there in the pouring rain.

'Darren. What the hell?'

'Thank God I've found you at last, Dan. It's mum. She's... she died.'

'Dead? How? I mean when?'

'Three days ago. Sorry. I didn't cope very well. I called the police when I found her dead in bed and-'

'What? You involved the *police*?' Alarm bells are ringing in Daniel Dee's head.

'Stupid, I know. But I was in a right state. Anyway, the community support officer was great. She contacted our doctor and he issued the death certificate. She also arranged for an undertaker to take mum's body. Since then I've spent most of the past two days trying to track you down.'

For Daniel, his mother's death is no big deal. But if his brother can find him then so could others. He needs to move on, and fast.

'Thanks for letting me know,' Daniel says.

'Can I come in?'

'What for? I've got to go out shortly.'

'*Daniel!* Our mum's just died. I haven't seen you for nearly twelve years. You could at least spare a few minutes to discuss the funeral arrangements.'

'Look, I've only got a hundred quid. I can let you have fifty towards the costs, and I'm happy to leave the details to you.'

Darren sighs. Ten years ago he had moved back to the family home to care for his mother. He had taken on all the housework, helping his mum to wash and dress before he went to work and then cooking the evening meal before putting her to bed. Eventually he had to give up the lease on his cycle-repair workshop and nurse his mum through what turned out to be the last two months of her life. By the time the old lady died Darren had used up most of his savings. He hoped to find another unit to rent and restart his business, but that would require every penny he could scrape together. He really needs his brother to step up and contribute.

'I really need to talk with you,' Darren says. 'So, are you going to keep me standing out here in the pouring rain?'

After a quick glance up and down the street Daniel says, 'Okay, if it's absolutely necessary.'

The brothers step into the hallway, where the only ornament is an oval mirror hanging incongruously on the grubby magnolia wall. Through an open doorway Darren can see into a cramped kitchen-dining room with a small plastic table and one chair.

'I live and work upstairs mainly, bro. You'd better come up. Oh... and mind you don't trip over the extension cable on the landing. There's no power socket in the bedroom.'

Daniel slumps into the only chair, leaving his brother to perch on the edge of the bed.

'It's... well, so spartan,' Darren says. 'I had no idea...'

'It's got everything I need, bro. And it's cheap. I'm only renting the place.'

'Okay, well, the point is, Daniel... the funeral's going to cost us eighteen hundred pounds.

'*What?* Bloody hell, bro. That's ridiculous!'

'It's the cheapest option I can find. Other than direct cremation, and we really can't do that. Mum always said she wanted to have a church service with hymns.'

'I haven't got that sort of money to waste on... No. No way!'

'I had rather hoped that *you* would cover the funeral costs this time, Dan. Remember, it was me who paid for dad's funeral. And it's me who burned through most of my savings looking after our mother these last couple of months.'

'Isn't that what social services are supposed to be for?'

Darren raises his eyebrows in a gesture of despair.

'Anyway,' Daniel says quickly, 'what about your bike shop? And that flat of yours. You still own those, don't you?'

'I've had to close my cycle repair business. It was only in a rented business-starter unit. I sold the attic flat years ago, to pay off mum's mortgage when I moved back to live with her after her stroke.'

'Didn't even know she'd had a stroke,' Daniel retorts. 'Nobody tells me *anything*.'

'It wasn't for the want of trying. You would have known about it if you'd kept in touch. If you'd been to see us once in a while. And by the way, the stroke was more than ten years ago.'

'That long? Well... I've been busy.'

'Doing what?' Darren asks.

'Helping people to set up new business ventures. That sort of thing.'

'The kind of help *I* could have done with years ago,' Darren mutters. 'And still need now.' He gets to his feet. 'We're never going to see eye to eye, are we, Dan? I can see I'm just wasting my time.'

Daniel Dee stares at the ceiling for a few moments and then makes a decision. 'Okay, bro. You go and make the arrangements, and I'll come round to the house tomorrow with the cash to pay for the funeral. I'll find the money somehow. But right now I need to go and see a client, or there won't *be* any money.' He stands up and pointed to the stairs. 'After you, bro...'

~~~

Community Support Officer Karen Chorley has no trouble finding the house. Only a few weeks ago she had been called to a sudden death there. An old lady with a history of health issues. Natural causes. But the son, her carer, had been in a terrible state. Karen pressed the doorbell, and as a key turned in the lock she frowned. The poor chap is about to have another bad day.

'Hello, Mr Dee. Can I come in please? It's about your brother.'

'Daniel? What's he done? He's not in trouble, is he? Sorry... come on through to the lounge.'

'I'm very sorry to tell you, but your brother is dead.'

The man sits down quickly and holds his head in his hands. 'Dead? How? Where? I mean... I don't even know where he lives. Lived.'

'I'm so sorry for your loss, Mr Dee. Really sorry. And coming so soon after the death of your mother. I'll just give you a few moments to get over the shock. Can I get you a cup of tea or something?'

'No. I'm okay. It's just... well, as you say, a shock. We were never close. When mum died I tried to contact him, for the funeral, but I failed. So, what happened? Had he been *ill*?'

'Your brother was found dead in a rented apartment on the other side of the city. An unfortunate accident. He'd fallen down the stairs and broken his neck. He wouldn't have suffered, I'm told.'

'Well, I suppose that's one small comfort.'

The PCSO nods and takes out her notebook. 'So where and when did you see you brother last.'

'Oh... here, actually. It must have been about 12 years ago. Just after dad died. There was nothing to suggest he had a drink problem, though. Not then, at least.'

'Nor now,' Karen replies. 'Seems pretty clear that he tripped on an extension lead connected to a portable heater. The cable was still hooked around one of his ankles.'

The man sighs and nods but says nothing.

'Before he can be cremated,' Karen continues, 'I'll have to ask you to identify the body. We believe he'd been lying there for three to four weeks before his landlady found him, so I'm afraid it's not going to be...'

'It's all right. Please... I just want to get it over and done with.'

As they are leaving the house, Karen notices the *For Sale by Auction* sign. 'Not planning on staying here, then?'

'Too many sad memories. Dad, mum, and now my brother as well. And anyway, this place is too big for me on my own. I'll probably rent somewhere, for a while at least.'

'Like your brother did,' Karen says. 'I can understand that.'

Oh no you can't, he thinks.

~~~

Returning from the morgue, the last surviving member of the Dee family closes the front door and smiles contentedly. The handsome face in the oval mirror on the wall smiles back at him, but then tears begin running down the cheeks. Red tears. Blood? Grabbing his handkerchief he wipes his eyes. The white handkerchief remains clean and dry. He blinks and again stares into the mirror. An unsmiling face stares back, no sign of bloody tears. Imagination playing tricks? Puzzled, he tries to remember. No, he can't recall seeing a mirror there earlier. Instinctively he raises his right hand and strokes his stubbly chin. The man in the mirror does likewise. Heading for the kitchen, he pulls up short in the doorway. Something's still bothering him. He goes back and stares into the mirror, and his reflection stares back reassuringly. He shrugs, and his reflection shrugs too.

~~~

The morning after his brother's cremation, he makes himself a coffee and sits in the kitchen. The furniture clearance van is due shortly, and then the house will be auctioned. Darren Dee is booked into a Travel Lodge for the next two nights, and then he is due to fly off to the beautiful villa in Barbados that he has just inherited. But he's pretty sure that, as usual, after a month or two he will want to come back and carry on just as before.

He glances at the kitchen clock. His reflection in the glass glowers at him. Puzzled, he goes back to the mirror in the hall. An angry face stares out at him, and instinctively he raises a fist to it. The reflection also raises a fist, and then thrusts it towards his face. He lurches away, but his reflection merely grins. Clean shaven with no hint of a moustache or the stubbly start of a goatee, the phantom face in the mirror is goading him to retaliate. Again instinctively, as he did as a boy whenever his 'so kind and helpful' twin stood up to him, he head buts the ghostly spectre, and it vanishes forever.

~~~

'We was given a key so we could clear the place,' the van driver said, his face white as a sheet, 'so we went straight in and found… this.'

PCSO Karen Chorley was on her afternoon round of visits when the two men in blue boiler suits had flagged her down. Now she stood staring at a body sprawled in the narrow hallway. From the way he was lying it was pretty obvious that the poor man had broken his neck when he fell, his head smashing against the bottom step of the stairs. Much harder to explain were the long spikes of broken mirror protruding from the sightless eye sockets.

-ooOoo-

21 A Grave Mistake

Martha Dudley reminded her husband that it was Cyril's fortieth. Could it really be forty years since he'd been moved in next door? A lifetime ago forty years might have seemed like an eternity, but now it was barely a blink. Such a strangely inappropriate expression, 'next door,' Ken Dudley realised. Like them, Cyril Climpley would never again see the great outdoors. Or meet anyone new. But in his mind's eye Cyril could still see everyone he'd ever met - Ken was well aware that. But mostly, of course, Cyril would be concentrating on the minutiae of his *own* life, blind to the issues of the day, giving his neighbours barely a second thought.

The Dudleys were equally inward looking. They had been in a terrible state when their old house had burned down. With no landlines up there on the moor, a mobile phone had seemed like a good investment at the time. In case of emergencies, Ken had told Martha. Leaving it permanently on charge in the spare bedroom had been a terrible mistake, though. By the time the smoke alarm woke them up, the fire had taken hold and there was no way of getting to the phone to call the fire brigade.

That was all so long ago, but it still seemed like only yesterday. Now, lying together in the dark, Ken and Martha Dudley could only imagine how poor old Cyril must be feeling, his wife being stuck miles away and having no living relatives to visit him. At least our Jamie and Celine had visited us when they were able to, Ken reminded his wife, and Celine always brought flowers. Nice girl. A tad serious for some folks' liking, perhaps, but she had been kind, caring, competent. Just right for our Jamie, Martha had said. Forward looking, too. While still relative youngsters, Celine had suggested to Jamie that they should buy a nice plot in southern France, and they were now firmly settled in there.

Ken and Martha would not want to be in Cyril's position. His wife had been miles away with her parents for what must seem an age, leaving the poor man here on his own, sandwiched between the Dudleys and a busy main road. Ken feels sure there must have been a grave mistake on somebody's part. Not our problem, though, he muses. There's nothing we can do. Except to carry on recycling responsibly, of course.

Martha agrees. She returns to the thought that had been running through her mind earlier that day. Or was it that night? Anyway, while wrapping Jamie's first birthday present – not that a one year old would have had any expectations – she fumbles the knot, breaks a fingernail (left forefinger) and swears. 'Damn!' Try again, and again… She *will* get past this cursed knot, eventually, and on to what comes next, but she also knows that she will have to come back to that infernal knot again. And again, and…

-oo0oo-

22 A Tissue of Truths

Emily enjoyed her walks on the common. Up the grassy slope from the village, along a short track through the woods and then down into the broad basin of Cartwell Common with its majestic trees, boating lake and colourful swings, slides and roundabouts. There was always so much to see, and with the woods now carpeted in bluebells interspersed with patches of wood anemones, her spirits had really been lifted. Early May and not a cloud in the sky. It was such a relief to forego the raincoat, scarf and gloves. Emily hated winter, which in her part of Lancashire sometimes spanned October to April with barely a glimpse of the sun. Today, with barely hint of a breeze, a sun hat might have been a good idea. She glanced at her watch: only twelve fifteen, and she had already walked nearly three miles. She needed a breather before setting off home, though, so she headed for her favourite lake-side bench.

The Common was buzzing with the happy chatter of picnickers all crammed together in the shade of the trees. Unbridled laughter and occasional screams came from children on the playground equipment. In contrast, the lake itself was an oasis of tranquillity. If you come via the woods and visit only the picnic area or the playground, you'd never know there *was* a lake, Emily mused. Low bushes – willows mostly – formed an almost continuous screen around the margin, but here and there strips had been left clear for benches, each with a small gravelled platform where people could feed the ducks. On one side of Emily's favourite resting place, a bench *"In memory of Carol and Bernie Hubbard, who loved Cartwell Lake,"* chaffinches and greenfinches sheltered in a dense hawthorn bush whenever the sparrow hawk was around. Once, while Emily was watching carp gulping bread missed by the ducks, a redwing had dropped in to pick up ripe red berries, a treat for its youngsters. Another tick on the bird-spotting list that she never quite got round to writing down.

Just before reaching 'her spot', Emily pulled up abruptly. A young woman was sitting in the middle of the bench, talking. Using a hands-free phone, Emily assumed.

'Sorry,' Emily said instinctively. I really must stop apologising whenever something unexpected happens, she told herself as she set off towards the next bench.

'Wait!'

Emily turned. The young woman had shuffled along to one end of the bench. 'Don't go, please. There's plenty of room.'

'I… I didn't want to intrude on your phone call. There's loads more benches. But… if you're sure.'

'Of course.'

'Emily,' she said as she settled onto the bench. 'Emily Franks.'

'Pru Taverner,' the young woman replied. 'My daughter loves it here. She gets a chance to play with other kids. On the swings and all that. She's an only child. It's really important to learn to mix, don't you agree?'

Emily smiled and nodded. If only I *had*, she thought.

'Oh, and don't worry, I wasn't on the phone,' Pru continued. 'I was just telling Tracey to keep away from the water. She never feels the cold and just loves getting muddy.'

Emily looked around. There was no sign of anyone else.

'Tracey will be with Brenda now,' Pru added quickly.

Without even bothering to go and check, how could the woman be sure? But, not wanting to seem pushy or critical, Emily settled for something uncontentious. 'Er, how old is Tracey?'

'Nearly fifteen,'

'*What!* Oh, I'm sorry, but…' Then Emily found an escape hatch and went for it. 'I mean, you don't look anywhere near old enough to have a fifteen-year-old daughter.'

Pru threw her head back and laughed. 'My fault, sorry. I should have said… Tracey's our dog. A present for Brenda's fifth birthday, two years ago. Brenda says Tracey's her best friend ever. She'd always wanted a rescue dog. Poor old Tracey, she's a bit arthritic now, but so affectionate.'

In the ensuing silence Emily began to feel uncomfortable. Had she upset her new friend with her clumsy thoughtlessness? She plugged the gap with, 'What kind?'

'The dog? Good question. It was *supposed* to be a golden retriever, but it turns out Tracey's a golden hoarder. Whenever I find a stick to throw she hobbles off after it but always comes back empty-' Another belly laugh and then, 'Well, not handed, not pawed. Empty mouthed, I suppose I should have said.' They both laughed, Emily feeling more comfortable now.

'I've got a couple of sandwiches,' Pru said. 'Cream cheese and chutney. Would you like one? I really shouldn't eat both myself. Trying to lose weight, or at least to stop putting it on.'

'Oh, well then, yes thank you. It's very kind of-' Then Emily thought: Oh no! I've done it again, jumped in with both feet. 'Sorry,

Pru,' she said. 'I wasn't thinking. What about your daughter. Won't she be needing...'

Pru shook her head and chuckled. 'Brenda's already eaten. She never wants to waste a minute once we get here, so I always let her have her lunch in the car.'

'In that case, thanks very much, I really-'

Pru's phone rang.

'Hi Dad. What? Where are you? Yes of course. I'm in the park with Brenda and the dog, but I can get to you in... what... ten to fifteen minutes. Have the jump leads ready, okay?' Pru turned to Emily. 'I'm sorry, Emily. Dad's left his van lights on and the battery's flat. Again!' Pru raised her eyebrows. 'He needs a hand. Gotta dash... hope to see you again. Here in the park perhaps?'

'I'm sorry,' Emily said. 'I mean about your dad's car. Lovely to meet you, Pru.'

What a shame, she thought. I'd have liked a chance to get to know her better. And to meet her little girl and the dog.

Emily stared at the sandwich that Pru had left for her. Waste not, want not, she thought as she wrapped it in tissues and popped it into her tote bag before setting off for home.

~~~

'Wake up, Emily dear. Time to come in. It's gone one o'clock.'

'Uh? Oh, hello darling. Everything all right?'

Rick Franks settled himself beside his wife and looked across the little pond that they had made together more than 20 years ago. A wrought-iron gate at the end of the garden opened onto a rough track leading to the woods half a mile away. I do hope we'll be able to go there next year, maybe at bluebell time, he thought. He stared at the chunky plaster cast on his leg. One clumsy fall and their lives had been changed so dramatically. 'Yes,' he said with a sigh. 'I'm okay, Em. What about you? I know you love the garden, but you've been sitting in full sun without your hat for nearly three hours. That's more than enough.'

'Sorry, Rick. Yes, the pond's lovely, but I haven't been here all that time. I went for a long walk and met a really nice young woman. Pru something or other. Anyway, she's got a little girl. She was playing on the swings so I never saw her – the daughter I mean. Oh, and an arthritic old dog.'

'Like me, you mean.'

Emily grinned and nodded. Despite her own serious nature, Emily valued Rick's ability to make her laugh, especially when he was mocking his own foibles and failings.

'I only wish we could both go for long walks,' Rick continued. 'Anyway, when I get over the operation we should at least be able to go shopping together, and who knows? Maybe much more. But at least you've had some fresh air this morning. You know I'd have loved to be with you, relaxing by the pond, but the pollen level is really high. Anyway, I've been keeping an eye on you from the lounge window. You've had a lovely sleep, darling, so-'

'No, Rick,' Emily interrupted. 'It's *you* who must have dropped off. I've only been back a few minutes.'

'You were *asleep*, Em. I had to shake you to wake you.'

Emily frowned. 'Yes, I know that, but I'd only just dropped off. The walk to Cartwell Common and back was tougher than I expected, but I'm really glad I went. When you're better we must go back there together.'

'In your dreams, Em. Which is how you went there today. Either that or I've slept all morning and somehow still managed to complete most of today's cryptic crossword.'

Emily shook her head. 'I could see that you'd nodded off before I left. Otherwise I would have told you where I-' Emily paused and stared into the distance. 'Oh.' She frowned. The crossword usually took them a couple of hours, and sometimes much more. Doubt trickled into a corner of her mind, and within moments it had torn a breach and now came flooding in. 'Well, I suppose it *could* have been a dream. Must have been, I suppose. But it's all so vivid. It's just not like me to remember dreams clearly. Once I wake up, they're usually just vague fragments.'

'Obviously not today,' Rick Franks said, placing a comforting hand on hers. 'Come on, Em. Let's go inside and get some lunch. Then you can help me with the last three cryptic clues.'

'Okay, I'll get the-'

'Aah...' Rick Franks sneezed five times in rapid succession.

'Oh, heck. Hay fever. I need a handkerchief.'

He tried to stand up, but Emily had hold of his sleeve. 'There's plenty of tissues in my tote bag,' she said. She held the bag out to her husband. 'Help yourself.'

'Aah...' Rick Franks grabbed a handful of tissues and sneezed into them.

'Yuck! What the hell?'

Emily began to giggle. Her husband was wearing a cheese and pickle face pack. 'Come on,' she said. 'Let's go in and polish off what's left of that crossword before lunch. Something tells me it's so easy that you could almost do most of it in your sleep.'

-ooOoo-

23 Sales Pressure

'Sorry to keep you waiting, sir... I'm having a spot of bother with our system. It says barcode not valid. Can't be, of course. I'll have to key in the ISBN manually... no, that doesn't work either. It's weird.'

Trainee sales assistant Greg Pilcher is in a quandary. The last thing he wants to do is to disturb his manager again. Maxine has been continuously tied up with trade reps, and he's interrupted her twice already this morning. 'Ah... I think I know what the problem is,' he says. 'Someone must have put your book into stock without recording its ISBN and recommended retail price.'

'Six quid,' the man says quickly. 'It's printed on the back cover. But it's *your* book until I buy it, and surely it's part of your job to know your system.'

'Yes, of course, sir. I'm not suggesting it's your mistake. It's ours, obviously. Possibly mine. New to the job and still learning. Sorry.'

'So I can't buy this book here, then? I'll have to go to another bookshop, is that it?'

Now Greg is really rattled. I'm barely a week into a new job, he thinks. It's hardly surprising things go wrong, but if this chap gives us a lousy online review Maxine will know it's my fault. So, what to do, then? Keep the customer waiting until the boss is free, or until he runs out of patience and storms off? Or use a bit of initiative? No contest!

Just to play safe Greg decides to check with Aileen, who is serving someone at the other till.

'Best not to bother Maxine unless you really have to,' Aileen says.

'Problem sorted, sir. Oh... do you need an itemised receipt?'

'Just the bloody *book*,' the man says irritably, glancing at his watch.

'Certainly, sir.' Greg puts the sale through as three ballpoint pens. He glances at the customer's credit card. 'Thank you, Mr Swallow. That'll be six pounds exactly.'

The man slides the bank card back into his wallet, pockets the purchase and hurries out.

～～～

'Hi Greg! How was your morning?' Aileen Courtney waves for her new colleague to bring his sandwiches over and join her. 'Shop's always frantic on Fridays, especially when a wet weekend is forecast.'

'Thanks Aileen. Yes, not bad. I mean pretty good, really.' Greg Pilcher pauses, then adds, 'But thanks for your advice earlier. At least I know I wasn't doing something stupid. That book just would *not* scan. Anyway, I put it through as stationery of the same value. Will that cause a problem?'

Aileen smiles. 'With the boss, you mean? No. As long as you made a note of the book title and ISBN so we can reorder it.'

'I did,' Greg says, showing her a Post-It containing the details. '*Mayhem in Mayfair* by A J Swift. 'It was our last copy.'

'It's definitely not something you were doing wrong. I had exactly the same problem with that title twice this morning. Leave it to me. I can put it right on the system, and they're obviously going to fly off the shelf so I'll suggest to Maxine that we need at least a couple of dozen copies. We're coming into the silly season. The run up to Christmas, I mean.'

~~~

Anthony J Swallow checks his emails. Excellent! Another really good order. His next trip out will be to drop three copies of *Mayhem in Mayfair* into Beaumonts Bookshop in Cramley-Wolverton, have a leisurely browse and then buy himself a copy. But that will have to wait until tomorrow. Right now A J Swift needs to make some progress with the sequel, *Mayhem in Marylebone.*

-ooOoo-

24 Flying Forever

The wooden clogs were too small for him, but by going without socks Roy Hedger could still just squeeze his feet into them. He wore them whenever he wanted to practice flying; no other shoes would do. He hoped that when he got much better at it he would be able to fly wearing ordinary shoes, but it was the clogs that had got him started, and so far nothing else seemed to work. He felt excited every time he put on those scruffy old clogs.

Roy's clogs didn't take him to places that would normally be out of bounds, and the excitement certainly didn't come from speeding along looking down on the world. He flew at little more than walking pace, skimming along so close to the ground that no one ever noticed that he *was* flying. This made it easy to keep his special talent a secret, but it also meant that he had to avoid rough ground, kerbs, potholes and the like. Steps were a definite no-no. ('Royston,' his mum would call from the kitchen. 'Don't wear those noisy clogs on the stairs, there's a good boy.') But on the level - along the pavement, on the lawn, and best of all when the playing fields had just been mown and no one else was around - Roy perfected his flying skills, gradually lengthening his stride and touching down ever more briefly until his special kind of flying became almost effortless. Best of all, at night when everyone else was asleep, he was in heaven. He could practice gliding silently along, gradually increasing the gaps between touchdowns – five, ten, fifteen, twenty seconds. He didn't have a watch, so he had to count in his head. His dad had told him that one day soon a runner was going to break the four-minute mile barrier, so Roy set himself a target too. He would try to break the four-minutes-between-touchdowns barrier. Night after night he kept trying, flying, counting in his head, but he always fell asleep long before reaching two hundred and forty.

Those old clogs, now five sizes too small for him, were hanging on the bedroom door, as they had done for more than three-quarters of a century. Lucy still had her mother's tattered teddy and a few other keepsakes from childhood, so she had had no problem sharing their home with her husband's most cherished possession.

Almost everything else in the bedroom had changed. A divan had replaced the old iron bedstead with its polished brass knobs. Fitted wardrobes and an en-suite shower and toilet now filled the tiny box room that had once been fancifully described as a third bedroom. And the flickering gas lamps that lit the rooms when Roy was learning to fly had long ago been ripped out to make way for several generations of ever more efficient electric lighting. All this made the bedroom so much more comfortable than the hospital ward he had just left. If I have to be ill, Roy mused, this is as fine a sick room as anyone could wish for. Lucy had just tucked him into bed. She would be back soon with his tablets and a hot drink.

Roy Hedger glanced lovingly at the old wooden clogs, smiled, and switched off the bedside light. Time to dream again. Time to fly again. One, two, three… …two hundred and thirty-nine, two hundred and forty. Made it, finally! No need to count any more. No need to touch down either. He was in heaven, flying forever.

-oo0oo-

25 Blue Screen of Death

'You're a B Sod, Ivan Costello, and I hate you.' Those were her last words to him before she departed, and they still reverberate in his head like an eternal echo. He has been on his own for two days, but still she won't leave him alone. Day and night he is under attack from the Nagging Nora in his head, never interesting, not even entertaining, just… there, uninvited, unwanted and unsilenceable.

Nora's repertoire had always been limited, but she made up for it by repetition. Most of her sentences began with, 'The trouble with you/him/her/them is…' or 'That's no use because…' or 'Some stupid idiot's just gone and…' A stream of never-ending negatives. Nothing was ever right. No one was any good. Especially him. Nothing he did, nothing he said ever made her happy. She was not short of wants, but reality always fell so far short of her expectations. He couldn't remember his wife ever having a good word for anyone. Her only blind spot, Ivan had quickly realised, was Nora Costello herself, who she deemed to be perfect and whose life and attainments were continually marred and thwarted by the inadequacies of others. She was the ultimate defect detective. Ivan was sure she would have found flaws in the silver lining of cloud nine. But that's not where she was.

Her last big "want" had been a large-screen TV. Ivan had been perfectly satisfied with the old grey box that sat on a small cupboard in the corner of the sitting room of their second-floor flat. A flat, he reminded himself, that Nora had said would be so much better than the bungalow he had inherited from his folks. Ivan had given up the garden he had so lovingly nurtured, the model railway in the attic, the golf course within walking distance, all in a desperate attempt to stem the diatribe of denigration. Like all previous attempts to placate his wife, this latest endeavour now seemed destined to fail. A flat with a sea view had done nothing to stem the litany of lament. At a price he could just about afford, *of course* the place needed a bit of work, but for someone with practical skills that wasn't an insurmountable problem. But fog was! They were on the east coast, and when the fog rolled in there was no sea view. Ivan couldn't do anything about that.

'Instead of just staring out at the fog for hours on end, why don't you find something you enjoy doing?' Ivan had said. His suggestion had not helped gone down well.

'If you weren't so mean we would have a large-screen TV above the fireplace. Instead all I can do is sit and stare at crumbling plaster, peer into a cracked mirror and watch paint peeling off the picture rail. Or squint at that flickering relic in the corner.'

'It's a colour telly, Nora. That's what you said you wanted.'

'Colour? Oh, yes… foggy blue. Makes everybody look like zombies. It makes me feel ill.' And with that she had turned the set around and sat staring sullenly at the faded label on the back. '*Made in England*… that dates it. *And* it was second hand, of course. Someone else's unwanted junk. Call yourself a Jack-of-all-trades… you never do *anything* nice just for me. Too busy pandering to your precious customers. How about a bit of *Charity Begins at Home* for a change?'

'You're like a spoilt child,' Ivan snapped. 'Never satisfied.' He had a hammer in his hand and he waved it at her threateningly.

'Just you try it, you pathetic little worm, and I'll come down on you like a ton of bricks.'

That had been the clincher. Ivan Costello had swung into action. Having drawn out the last of his savings, he had driven straight down to Johnson Brothers to buy the biggest TV they had in stock. It was an ex-display model, so Craig Johnson had given him 20% discount and a free wall fixing kit. He had also offered to come over and check the wall to make sure it was suitable for such a heavy load.

'The brickwork and plaster where you mount the bracket needs to be really sound,' Craig had explained. 'Otherwise there's a serious risk of this beast falling off the wall. The heavy-duty fixing bolts have to go right through into the cavity, so if the mortar's knackered it's not just the TV and the bracket but the whole wall that lands on your head. But don't worry. For an extra £200 you can have an expert survey, and if the wall is okay Carl and I can install it there and then. And we would set up the channels for you.'

'I'm a builder,' Ivan had replied. 'If the wall's not sound I'll rebuild it and replaster before I fix the TV. And I had no trouble setting up our present TV.'

In one last attempt at up-selling, Craig Johnson had offered him a two-year extended warranty for *only* an additional 50% of the price of the TV.

Ivan's credit card was nearly maxed out. 'No thanks. But If I have any trouble tuning in the programmes can I call you for help? Help over the phone, I mean.'

'You can certainly do that,' Craig had replied as he helped Ivan load the huge package into the builder's van.

~~~

Ivan had stood there, beaming proudly. 'How about this then, Nora?'

Nora Costello stared at the huge carton that was leaning against the fireplace. 'Resolution 1080P… is that all?'

'It means high definition, Nora,' Ivan had said. 'So what's wrong *now*?'

'Not Utra HD, then? Not 8K… not even 4k. You've been sold a pup, Ivan. Big screen but with an ugly fat bezel. I'll bet it's a discontinued model. Obsolete tech being flogged off cheap.'

That was the last straw. Ivan had dragged the TV out of its box and turned its face to the wall. 'Look at all those lovely labels on the back, Nora. You'll enjoy staring at those, I'm sure. HDMI1, HDMI2, Antenna In, USB Out. Those are just the headlines. Read on. There's lots more in the small print.'

~~~

Thump, thump, thump! Miss Bright was banging her broom on the ceiling of her bedroom, which was also Ivan's sitting-room floor. She did that whenever his DIY extended beyond 5pm, even something as simple as putting up a shelf. He had listened politely to her catalogue of ailments and those of her pongy poodle before informing her that he had to do some essential repair work but would be as quiet as he possibly could and, of course, only work between the hours of nine and five. A peace offering in the form of bottle of cream sherry had given him two evenings when he could work as late as he wanted while the old bag was comatose. Now that the sherry bottle was empty the five-o'clock thumping had resumed. But Ivan was prepared. Clasping a second bottle of sherry, he headed down to Miss Bright's floor and knocked at her door.

With a much-practised glower at the ready, Amanda Bright opened the door in her shaggy housecoat. A cursory glance at Ivan Costello's right hand quashed any complaints. 'Oh, Mr Costello, that really isn't necessary,' she said, reaching for the bottle and cradling it carefully in both hands. 'Do come in. Can I offer you a little something? A sherry, perhaps? I'm afraid I haven't anything stronger.'

'No, really. I just wanted to thank you for being so understanding. I've nearly finished the repair work, so you'll soon have peace and quiet.'

'The bashing and banging all day, or the scratching and scraping all night?'

Ivan frowned. Taking down the old wall, removing the fireplace and rebuilding the wall had been two long days' work and unavoidably noisy, but he had made it a rule to stop at midnight.

'The wall above our fireplace was close to falling down,' he said, 'but it's more or less sorted now. All I've got to do is a bit of plastering and drill some fixing holes. Nora wanted a TV on the wall, so while she's away I thought it would be nice to get that sorted.'

'She's lucky to have you, Mr Costello. When's she coming back?'

'It's all a bit up in the air at present, what with her cousin being taken ill and there being no one else to look after his aquarium. Tropical fish. They need so much attention.'

Amanda Bright nodded. 'You must be lonely,' she said, smiling coyly and holding out a hand.

Not that lonely, Ivan thought, backing towards the door. 'Sorry,' he said. 'I've gotta dash. I left my power drill on charge.'

Miss Bright shrugged and turned back to the full bottle of sherry on her kitchen table. At least she would get a good night's sleep. She would get plastered, and Ivan Costello could do as much plastering as he liked. No amount of scratching and scraping was going to keep her awake tonight.

~~~

Once the quick-set plaster has hardened, Ivan Costello drills holes for the four long bolts that will secure the TV mounting bracket. Each hole goes right through the brickwork and into the chimney breast cavity of the old Victorian edifice. Then, with the bracket installed he manhandles the massive TV into position using a makeshift arrangement of kitchen chairs, ropes and step ladders. The TV clicks into place and Ivan stands back to admire his work. Dead central, dead level… dead cinch! He clears away the tools and plugs in the aerial and mains cables. The 32-page handbook looks a bit daunting. No, he tells himself, just comprehensive. Start at the beginning…

Ivan glances up at the screen. A bright yellow egg timer is rotating on a dark blue background, and then words appear: *'Setting up your new TV… Scanning for Channels… please wait.'* Ivan waits. *'Found 87 Channels… set-up complete.'* That was a doddle, he thinks. Not worth £200, that's for sure. Now what? Page 1 of the handbook shows a picture of the contents of the box. TV, the two cables, and a remote control unit. He tips up the box and out falls the missing item. Ivan grabs it and presses button 1. Moments later a weather forecaster appears saying, "…except for the east coast, where tomorrow morning's fog may be slow to clear and in sheltered coves might persist well into the afternoon."

Ivan clicks through half a dozen channels. All working perfectly. Bloody brilliant! He channel hops until, on channel 63, he finds that *For Your Eyes Only*, an old James Bond film, is due to start in ten minutes. Perfect. He will make himself some cheese sandwiches, crack open a beer and drag in the duvet. Ivan is looking forward to a relaxing, nag-free evening of high-definition entertainment. 'For my eyes only,' he mutters contentedly.

~~~

Roger Moore is in dire peril in a skating rink when suddenly the TV screen turns blue. Ivan sits bolt upright. *It's brand new. Surely it can't be-* But then the screen flickers, and against the foggy blue background he sees a pale shrouded figure lying prone on a stone slab. Slowly the spectre sits up and turns its face towards Ivan. Except there isn't a face. Just bandages, with black holes where the eyes and mouth should have been.

Ivan's idea of exciting entertainment involves car chases, helicopter crashes, murder and mayhem. What he can't abide are ghoulies and ghosties and long-legged beasties. So why has his new TV switched itself to a Hammer Horror film? He checks the channel number in the top left-hand corner of the screen. Number 666. That's devilishly weird. Only 87 channels were found, so where did this come from? A glitch? Ivan knows that modern TVs are basically digital computers, which are far from infallible. The problem is easily fixed by pressing 63 on the remote. Bond is back and with the girl on his arm. Ivan lets out an expletive. He has missed the big shootout. Still, let's see what's next up. Yes… another action movie. He cracks open a second can of beer, takes a sip and lies back on the sofa. But even before the credits roll, the TV screen turns blue again and The Mummy is back, waving its arms menacingly. That's scary. Ivan presses the off switch and the spectre vanishes. The automatic setup must have gone seriously awry. It's too late now, but tomorrow morning he will phone Craig Johnson and get help. Meanwhile, he'll just finish his beer before hitting the hay.

Then comes an even bigger shock. The TV screen flickers and glows blue. The Mummy reappears, bashing its bandaged fists against the front of the screen and letting out high-pitched screams that make Ivan's flesh crawl. He eyes the beer can with suspicion, shakes his head and tries to think. *Think!*

Got it! There must be enough electricity stored in the TV to keep it going for a while. Maybe there's a small internal battery to make it immune to brief power blips. Answer: unplug the aerial lead. Sorted! The screen goes black and the screaming stops. Ivan takes another big swig of his beer. He can feel his heart rate returning to normal. Time for bed.

~~~

It's pitch black, sometime in the early hours, but Ivan Costello isn't asleep. Something has woken him up. A scraping noise coming through the wall. Could there be an intruder in his sitting room? He is pretty sure he locked the front door, the only door into the flat. Nora called it paranoia, but he has always double checked before going to bed, just in case.

Grabbing the heavy metal torch that hangs beside the bed in case of power cuts, Ivan opens the bedroom door and creeps cautiously into the sitting room. It is no longer in darkness. A flickering blue glow illuminates the sofa, the reclining chairs, the sideboard, the coffee table. Ivan swings his torch around the room. 'I'm warning you,' he says. His attempt to sound threatening is not helped by a mouth as dry as dust and the uncontrollable quavering of his voice. But there is no one in the room. The light is coming from the TV. The Mummy now has a hammer and is bashing the screen so hard that it visibly shakes. With its other hand the ghoulish spectre continues scratching and scraping as though trying to clear away the debris created by the hammer.

Ivan Costello shuts his eyes and holds his hands over his ears. In the silent darkness he tries to think. What has he done to deserve this? But he knows the answer, and he is sure something terrible will happen if The Mummy shakes the fixing bolts out of the wall. Ivan drops to the floor and shines his torch up behind the TV. As he feared, the bracket *is* coming loose. The two lower bolts fall to the floor either side of him, and he stares transfixed as the upper bolts pull free of the brickwork. As if in slow motion, he sees the massive black screen descending towards his head. He fends it off with his fists and laughs victoriously as the TV hits a corner of the coffee table and shatters into pieces. The Mummy lets out a strangulated scream and the room falls silent. Ivan has beaten the beastly phantom. The room is now lit only by yellow torchlight. Although it's a mess, it's nothing he can't fix.

But before he can pick himself up, the banging noises return. Ivan Costello stares in horror as his new wall cracks and collapses outwards, and he can only watch as a ton of bricks descends towards his head.

~~~

'There… installed and ready to go. Wifi enabled. Linked to your new mobile phone and your iPad. All the very latest tech *and* an extra two-years warranty. You're all set up now. No worries.'

'Thank you. That's excellent.'

'Er… just one thing. The brickwork and plastering… well… I mean, it's okay, but it's not quite what I'd expect of a professional builder.'

'It's not going to fall down this time. That's all that really matters. It won't be visible. My lovely new TV covers a multitude of sins. I'm not going to waste any time worrying about what's behind it.'

Craig Johnson smiles. 'You're quite right, of course. And as long as you're happy, we're happy.'

'It's a very long time since I've felt this happy, Mr Johnson. And to help me celebrate, my friend from downstairs is joining me for dinner this evening. Then there's a really good Hammer Horror film on at eight o'clock, so it'll be great to have company. A girls' night in.'

-oo0oo-

26 Feet of Clay

'If your adoring public only knew about your cruel and abusive side, Arnold, the adoring would be over. Overnight.'

'How can you say that, Carol? You and the kids… you owe *everything* to me. Call it playing with plasticine if you like, but it's me working flat out on my animated films that pays for all this. The flat, the flat-screen TV you say you had always wanted. We'd be flat broke if we had to rely on your contribution. Namely nothing.'

'I would if I could,' Carol said weakly.

Arnold sniffed. 'I said I'm sorry about your arm. It *was* clumsy, I admit. Out of character. A one off. Heavy handedness wouldn't have got me where I am today. It was an accident, but you've been milking it for quite long enough.'

'It's not about me, Arnold. It's about you and they way you treat us. The twins in particular.'

'Hang on a minute… You were homeless, Dumped and destitute, remember? *You* couldn't look after them. Who else would have taken you in and put up with your continual complaining. Though I say it myself, you're damn lucky to have me.'

Carol stared straight ahead. 'It's no life. Not for me and certainly not for them. You go out whenever you want to, but we're stuck here. I know it's a nice apartment with great views across the city. But we don't just want to see other people enjoying life. We want to be part of it. Why don't you ever take us out?'

Arnold Mulder made no reply.

'Did you treat your first wife this way? Is that why she left you?'

'My first and only wife. And no. I didn't break her arm, if that's what you mean.'

'But you bullied her, I'll bet. She left you for a reason. I reckon she walked out because you abused her. Yes, that's it. Just like you abuse me and the twins.'

'I've never laid a finger on the twins. You know that.'

Carol let out an exaggerated sigh. 'Not all abuse is physical, Arnold. The poor dears have never been on a bus, a train, a plane. Self schooling means they never get to meet other kids. You expect them to sit in silence waiting until you can find time to read to them or tell them stories. They're not tall enough to reach books from the shelf themselves, so they don't even get to choose. You decide *everything*.'

'They never complain. Not like you, Carol. Maybe you should take a leaf out of-' Arnold Mulder stopped himself. 'Sorry, I forgot. You can't. Not with a broken arm.'

Carol stared straight ahead but said nothing.

'Okay, okay,' Arnold Mulder said. 'I just want you to know that I *do* care. And to prove it I've made you a new arm. I'll fix it on now, and I'll try to be more careful in future.'

'Thank you, Arnold. I'm just putty in your hands. I do love you.'

-oo0oo-

27 Neither Friend Nor Foe

Renowned military strategist General Sir Maxwell Stoneycroft has faced and defeated many enemies - some preordained, others of his own making. The general has no fear of enemies. Friends, then? He knows better than to make any of those. Which only leaves family. And with his parents long dead and no siblings or other close relatives, that simply means… her. One stupid tactical error in an otherwise unblemished career. But that scary little skeleton could leap out of the cupboard at any time. He draws no comfort from "okay so far." It was never going to be his call. This solitary black cloud will always hang over his otherwise idyllic existence… unless he makes a pre-emptive strike.

A much-decorated war hero and knight of the realm, the general is always in great demand. In the two years since retiring, he has had more than a hundred after-dinner speaking engagements. He has also generously given up the occasional afternoon to cut ribbons or launch fund-raising appeals for high-profile worthy charities. His circle of influence continues to expand, as also do the funds in his coffers and, less welcome, his waistline, now clearly in conflict with an action-man image.

Never daunted by the prospect of conflict, two months ago General Stoneycroft had moved into action. The private nutrition clinic had sampled his DNA and produced a tailor-made diet matched precisely, they had assured him, to his specific metabolic needs. Their daily deliveries of delicious food made from finest and freshest ingredients were guaranteed to be entirely free from allergens and toxins. He could hardly fault the service. Well, they had got one small detail wrong: the portion sizes. That, he quickly realised, was easily fixed. He simply doubled the order, and the hunger pains melted away. Sadly, his waistline didn't, but having gone into battle he would stick to his guns. He was in this campaign for the long haul.

But then the nightmares started. That DNA sample. If *she* gained access to it, no longer would it be the word of a grasping something-for-nothing nobody against that of a prominent public figure with impeccable credentials. *"Do Not Argue,"* the judge was saying. *"DNA does not lie. Proof beyond doubt, therefore, that you General Maxwell Stoneycroft have lied under oath."* He would wake up in a cold sweat. The knighthood, those dinners and speaking engagements, his very existence… he stood to lose *everything*.

Thereafter the spectre of unbearable ignominy hung over his every waking moment and pervaded all his dreams. He needed to know where she was, who she was calling herself now, and what evidence, if any, she had. But then what to do about it? So many unanswered questions. He had no strategy, no tactics for this kind of thing.

In desperation, he sought the help of a private eye. Via a comparison website he had opted for someone with a military background. A big mistake. The unscrupulous rogue took the thousand-pound fee, made a few enquiries via ancestry websites, and reported that he had no known living relatives. He already knew that… it was the *unknown* one that haunted him.

And then out of the blue NFNF had contacted him about his 'failed search'. They wouldn't say how they knew, but they said the search had not been comprehensive and would he like them to investigate on a no-find no-fee basis. It was a no brainer. He would use NFNF to launch a surprise counter offensive. Which was why he had answered all of Safroc's seemingly irrelevant questions. Safroc, hiding behind a darkened glass window. Safroc the secretive. Or was he just unspeakably shy? Yes, that would explain why all the questions and answers had to be in writing.

Having emerged with flying colours from phase one, the skirmish with Safroc – with hindsight he rated it as barely a scuffle – the general had moved on to phase two of the campaign, which the NFNF brochure referred to as the contract-consultation stage. The contract consultant, a tall young woman who stood out from the crowd, as the general perceptively observed, not merely by dint of her height but more by an absence of tattoos and the presence of mind to go straight for the jugular, the money. He secretly approved of this.

'*How much?* That's a bit steep.' The general looked as if he was about to burst a blood vessel. And it might not be one of his own.

The consultant smiled. 'Yes, general. But if you want results, and quickly… five thousand pounds. Plus VAT at the standard rate. We have to charge VAT. It's the law, and an agency such as ours has to be squeaky clean. I'm sure you'll understand that. So…' the young woman clicked a mouse button and glanced at her computer screen. 'Including VAT that's six thousand, NFNF.'

'I thought NFNF was just the name of your agency thingy.'

'That's correct, general. It stands for *No Find No Fee*. It means-'

The retired military man leapt to his feet. 'Double negative! It's bloody obvious what it means. You're *expecting* to fail, just like that other idiot. Waste of time, waste of money. Private eye my foot! Turned out to be a brainless ex-squaddie who would never have progressed through the ranks. And now I find you're just a bunch of civvy-street idiots of similar ilk.'

'I assure you, general... we have a verified success rate of 99.9 per cent. Please also bear in mind that in the extremely unlikely event of us failing to find your missing relative it wouldn't cost you anything, apart from the ten minutes you have just spent answering Safroc's questions about yourself and the, er... missing person.'

'I see...' General Sir Maxwell Stoneycroft subsided into the overstuffed club chair, stroking his chin while his brain struggled to find a down side to the proposition. Finding down sides was his speciality, and he quickly countered with, 'How can you be *sure* of that figure? You would need to have had...' more chin stroking, this time a cover for simple arithmetic - not one of his strong points. 'Well, a huge number of successes.' Sensing that he was on to a winner, the general settled back, jutted out his chin and demanded, 'So? How many *have* you found, Mrs er...?'

'Doctor. Dr Clare Beynon.' Again the woman fiddled briefly with the mouse and checked her computer screen for the answer. 'Twenty thousand two hundred and forty-six, as of midnight yesterday.' She glanced at her smart watch, which was buzzing and flashing a message. 'Is there anything else you want to ask me before you make your decision, general?'

'Twenty thousand successes... Twenty thousand times five thousand pounds equals... successful to some extent, perhaps. But what about the failures? How many?'

'Twenty three,' Clare Beynon replied without relying on computer assistance. 'Twelve of them turned out to be dead. They all died during the few days between NFNF being given the search contract and the completion of our world-wide search and locate process. The other eleven are works in progress.'

'So, twelve total failures and you've no idea why. You must feel awfully sad about those failures. It must be enough to make you regret choosing this as a career.'

Dr Beynon sighed, 'Sad? Yes, I do feel sad about those twelve cases but not for the reason you imply. They were all murdered.'

General Sir Maxwell Stoneycroft's face lit up. '*Really?* Well, I can see how being implicated in unsolved murders must weigh on your mind. I'll bet it keeps you awake at nights.'

'As I said at the start of this consultation, I'm not at liberty to discuss the details of specific cases with you, general, just as I have promised never to disclose your personal information to another living person.

Subject to acting at all times in strict accordance with the laws of the land and our various contractual obligations, of course. Complete confidentiality is core to client satisfaction.'

The military man pondered the near-perfect alliteration and nodded pensively. 'Shame there's no C word for satisfaction,' he muttered. 'Contentment doesn't quite cut the mustard. But then, it never did.' He was wondering whether to add that too much mustard could cut the contentment when he became aware tht the consultant was waving her arms in a desperate attempt to regain his attention.

'What I *can* tell you, general, is that they are no longer unsolved murders.' The woman now had his full attention. 'In each of these cases we were able to use our search and locate system to identify and find the murderers. After anonymising all personal data other than those of the victims and perpetrators, we duly handed over all twelve case files to the appropriate authorities.'

'So you shopped the murdering bastards?'

Clare Beynon clicked and flourished her mouse several times before replying. 'I must correct you there, General Stoneycroft. Just seven of them turned out to have been born out of wedlock. I'm not at liberty to disclose their names. However, it's worth noting that of those seven only two had surnames beginning with Fitz.'

The general was suffering from information overload. 'Where were we before you went off on this tiresomely trivial tangent?'

'Six thousand pounds. Three thousand on signature of contract...' The consultant thrust forward a typed sheet of bond paper, her finger pointing to a dotted line. 'Here, please... and the balance upon co-location of client and sought persona.'

'And in *English*?'

'Three grand either in cash or via bank transfer right now. The other three grand here in my office next Monday morning when you have received satisfactory answers to the four questions listed in this contract and you can see that we have indeed located your long-lost relative. Or your three grand deposit returned in full, there and then, in the zero point one per cent chance that we should fail to find your relative, either because you have murdered him or her in the interim or because he or she became an astronaut, left the planet and has not yet re-entered earth's atmosphere. Clear enough?'

Although he gave it a brief try, not even General Sir Maxwell Stoneycroft could pick holes in that, at least none big enough to let through any light. He shrugged, placed a wodge of bank notes on the desk, picked up the silver NFNF ball-point pen and scribbled his signature above the dotted line.

The consultant picked up the wodge of notes, opened a desk drawer, and dropped it in.

'Not going to count them?'

'Exactly three thousand in used notes, as agreed,' she replied. Noticing her client's raised eyebrows she added, 'Six microseconds after you placed them on the desk, our surveillance system had scanned them, counted them, logged the serial numbers of each and checked their provenance. Crucial money-laundering countermeasures are a key step in our due diligence process. You can relax now, general, and leave it to NFNF to get on with the job. I'm just giving Safroc the instruction to... Seek – And – Find – Relative – Of – Client. There... done!' The consultant gave her mouse another good clicking and pointed towards a darkened glass wall. The general could just make out a middle-aged woman in a white lab coat who was sitting, apparently dozing, with a keyboard on her lap. 'Don't worry, it's a one-way mirror. Nothing you say in here gets out unless I release it, via my partner, to Safroc for the sole purpose of finding your missing relative and securing the outcomes detailed in our contract.'

The general stared at the darkened glass wall beyond which, on a large computer screen, columns of text and numbers were scrolling and periodically changing colours.

'That's where the real work is done,' the consultant explained. 'In that secure, climate-controlled room Safroc will be progressing your case, among others, throughout the weekend, surveying all legitimate archive data sources including the web, the dark web and the blackest of black webs. We're also geared up to hack hackers and recover any stolen data that's not rightfully theirs. But always operating within the laws of the land, while in each instance selecting the most favourable land from all the known lands on earth in order to maximise our effectiveness.' Dr Beynon paused, but getting no reaction she added, 'Naturally.'

'Naturally,' the general said instinctively, before realising that this sounded like agreement. As he couldn't disagree with something he had not the slightest chance of ever understanding, he finished with a lame, 'As you say.' But something must have registered, because before the consultant could intervene he added, 'Let me talk to this Safroc fellow. Until the job's done, I want him to work exclusively for me. I'm willing to pay a premium... say, an extra day's wages?'

'Safroc prefers the pronoun *they*,' the consultant said.

The general turned red in the face as the consultant continued, 'Have you any idea what a day of Safroc's time costs? I urge you to leave such decisions to the appropriate expert.' She noticed that her client was shaking his head. 'Oh, no. Not me. I was referring to Safroc. And I'm sorry, general, but Safroc is far too busy to see you today. Some other time, perhaps.'

'Bloody silly name,' was all that General Sir Maxwell Stoneycroft could come up with, but it was dawning on him that offering to shell out for an extra day of Safroc's time might have been a tad impetuous. 'Well, in that case,' he continued, 'I'll leave you to it. You and your precious Safroc and *their* anonymous sleeping partner.'

The sarcasm in the general's voice went ignored if not unnoticed. Dr Beynon smiled politely. 'Good. That's all settled, then. I'm 99.9 per cent certain I'll be able to see you here in my office at… what shall we say… 10.30 on Monday morning? And don't forget to bring the balance of our fee. In the meantime, have a nice relaxing weekend, and prepare yourself for an end to those nightmares about a long-lost blood relative.'

'One bloody relative is one too many,' the general muttered as he strode out of the office, shaking with rage at the thought of having been given the brush off by a *they*.

~~~

'*How much?*' Maxine Quinn looked as though she was about to pass out.

'Fifty thousand pounds. Plus VAT at the standard rate, so…' the younger woman clicked the mouse button and glanced at her computer screen. 'In total that's sixty thousand, NFNF.'

'But NFNF is the name of your agency. What else does it mean?'

'It *is* the name of our agency, Maxine. It stands for *No Funding-stream No Fee.*' The consultant's smart watched buzzed and she checked the message. 'Oh, good. Safroc has processed your DNA sample and I'm delighted to inform you that all is absolutely fine. Now, where were we? Oh yes, the contract. It means you risk absolutely nothing, and there's a 99.9 per cent chance of you securing a legacy of at least ten times our fee. But it also means there is one chance in a thousand of you realising that legacy *plus,* in due course, ninety per cent of a great deal money more if your wealthy blood relative passes away intestate this weekend.'

The client was looking very confused.

'Dies, I mean,' the consultant said.

The client nodded slowly but still looked a bit puzzled.

'Dies in the natural course of events, I should have said.'

'Ah, I see! So... one chance in a thousand that you'll murder the old bastard for me,' the client said, smiling broadly.

'Oh no, Maxine! Heaven forbid! We'd *never* do such a thing.'

The client's frown had returned, and the consultant sought to assuage her concern. 'No,' she went on quickly. 'I mean there's a chance in a thousand that we could *arrange* to have him murdered by someone who has, or at least is led to believe they have, some other sort of connection with him, namely a matter-of-life-and-death grudge to settle. But crucially, someone with not even the remotest connection with you. Or of course with us. NFNF, that is. Only when we are 99.999 per cent certain of that, and once all client data – yours in this instance - has been comprehensively anonymised... only then would we ever release Safroc's findings to the appropriate authorities.'

'The police, you mean.'

'In this case, yes.'

'And you say you've already found the bastard and unearthed whatever it is I'm supposed to have on him? Something he'll be willing to shell out half a million to keep under wraps for the rest of his days?'

The consultant nodded.

'And he's really got that sort of money?'

The consultant nodded again. 'So... fifty grand to be transferred from your relative's account direct to NFNF next Monday. Safroc already has the necessary bank details. That's ten percent of the funding stream. Likewise, the other ninety per cent going straight to your designated account. Again, Safroc has the details.'

Thrusting forward a typed sheet of bond paper, the consultant pointed to a dotted line. 'Just sign here, please, Maxine.'

The client picked up the silver NFNF ball-point pen and scribbled her signature above the dotted line.

'Thank you. I'm just giving Safroc the instruction to... **S**haft – **A**nd – **F**leece – **R**elative – **O**f – **C**lient. There... done!' The consultant gave her mouse another good clicking and pointed towards a darkened glass wall, behind which a middle-aged woman in a tweed suit sat, apparently dozing, with a sheaf of papers on her lap. 'Don't worry, it's a one-way mirror. Nothing you say in here gets out unless I release it, via my partner, to Safroc for the sole purpose of securing your relative's agreement to set up the aforementioned funding streams in your favour and in ours, as detailed in our contract.'

The office lights flickered briefly, and then the consultant smiled. 'Excellent. I'll see you at 10.30 on Monday morning, although as I've explained you won't be able to see me or your beneficiary, because you will be on the other side of the one-way mirror. Good afternoon, Ms Quinn.'

Maxine Quinn nodded and stepped towards the door. 'Oh... one last thing. Can I have a quick word with Safroc? I'd like to thank her personally.'

'Of course. On Monday, okay? But Safroc prefers the pronoun *they*.'

'Me too,' Maxine said. 'Until Monday, then.'

-oo0oo-

28 Fairy Tail-ending

Their council house was nothing special – two up, two down with an outside loo and gas lighting – but it had a very special garden for which, as his mum's arthritis got worse, young Richard gradually assumed responsibility. The first part that he took over, and by far the best bit, was what he called the wilderness. Beyond the herbs and the rows of potatoes, carrots, peas and beetroots, mostly grown from seed saved from previous years, wildflowers thrived. There was no spare cash for such non-essentials as garden furniture and ornaments, but that small patch of wilderness was home to something money could never buy. A fairy lived there, among the tangle of buttercups and bindweed, honeysuckle and hardheads. Many other weeds with names unknown to the six-year-old had also escaped cultivation in what to a budding botanist was a wildflower wonderland.

While weeding between the rows of vegetables, Richard would sometimes sense her presence and turn quickly, trying to catch a glimpse of his fairy friend. But she was shy. The boy understood shyness. Despite being one of the tallest in his class and the second fastest runner, he too found it hard to make friends - at least of the kind he yearned for. None of his schoolmates was the least bit interested in wildflowers. But the fairy was. Almost as tall as he was, she was slim with short blonde hair cupped over her head like an early spring buttercup. Her brick-red dress, the petals of scarlet pimpernel, flared and flounced as she darted back and forth like a damselfly.

But he did see the fairy for certain, not in the wilderness garden but at night when he was tucked up in bed, and most of all Richard loved her smile, like brilliant sunshine even on rainy days. The gas light on his bedroom wall didn't work, and his Wee Willie Winkie candle was strictly only for going upstairs, so he couldn't read in bed. Instead, he would tell stories to the wildflower fairy.

He would wait until the house fell silent and then, in a conspiratorial whisper, Richard would tell his fairy friend what he had found interesting that day at school or, more often, about the birds, insects, snails, flowers and anything else in the hedgerows surrounding the playground. She was always interested and would whisper questions in his ear, usually starting with *Why...* and *How...* and he would fall asleep trying to work out the answers. How do snails climb to tops of nettles and thistles without getting hurt? Why do some flowers close up early in the afternoon? By next morning the fairy had always gone, leaving him with yet more additions to the list of puzzles that he hoped one day to solve.

Richard was nearly eight when they moved to the new house, with electric lights and an inside toilet. He would readily have sacrificed reading in bed for the company of the wildflower fairy, but there was no wilderness at the bottom of the new, much smaller garden. Richard now did most of the gardening, and mum wanted as many vegetables as the plot could produce – no lawn, no flowerbeds either. But some nights, when Richard didn't read himself to sleep, the wildflower fairy still visited, sitting as always, on the pillow beside his head, listening to his stories and leaving him with yet more questions that he couldn't answer.

~~~

To young Richard looking forward, the period between approaching adolescence and encroaching senescence had seemed vast. Now, to an old man looking back, it had shrank to a few winks. Still with far more questions than answers, he lies in bed and ponders the wonders that have made yet another day unique, special, exciting. He turns to the flower fairy who, with her golden hair a little paler now but still shining and so very beautiful, lies on the pillow beside him.

"*I wonder why…*" she asks.

"*I wonder how…*" he replies.

And tomorrow, together, they will carry on looking for answers.

-ooOoo-

About the author

Writer and broadcaster Pat O'Reilly came from Bromsgrove - one of his better decisions, he claims. He worked hard but briefly as an electronics engineer, less hard and more briefly as a college and university lecturer, and hardly hard at all for more than thirty years as a fly-fishing instructor. He has also had lots of fun running writers' courses and as a management consultant specialising in mobilising imagination and creativity, while keeping his own feet firmly grounded as an environmental advisor to governments.

Pat O'Reilly has written more than thirty books and numerous newspaper and magazine articles. His most recent non-fiction work is a revised and enlarged second edition of the bestselling *Fascinated by Fungi*, published in 2016. Prior to the Winding River Mysteries trilogy of thrillers (2021 – 2023) his most recent novel, born in 2014, is the hilarious twin-world fantasy *Frazzle* – also now an Amazon Kindle publication.

Pat's hobbies include fly fishing, hiking, wildlife photography, and of course writing facts and fiction (striving to maintain some separation between the two) about these and other obsessions.

Awarded the MBE in 2003 for his environmental work, Pat O'Reilly lives in Wales with his wife Sue and far too many books. Pat and Sue are the authors of the 2500-page wildlife and ecology website first-nature.com

-ooOoo-

Printed in Great Britain
by Amazon